Ad Infinitum

unchanging and Forevermore

Michele Doucette

Ad Infinitum: Unchanging and Forevermore

ISBN 978-1-935786-54-2

Printed in the United States of America by

St. Clair Publications

PO Box 726

McMinnville, TN   37111-0726

http://stclairpublications.com/

Table of Contents

Dedication

To the many authors, orators and writers, from all walks of life, who continue to inspire me with their compositions, reflections, thoughts and words; may they also continue to remain steadfast to the truth of why they pen their words for all to read.

As always, my husband, Albert; after 29 years of dedication to each other, he remains my own special hero.

Author's Note

There are different time periods in history that stand out (resonate) for each person.

As an individual, with no past life memories, I can only take these experiences to mean that I have some personal connection to these time frames (as in having lived there, once upon a time).

Foreword

Delving into the life of Edgar Cayce, referenced as the Sleeping Prophet, I came across a book called <u>The Reincarnation of Edgar Cayce</u> by Wynn Free; a book that details the intriguing connection between Edgar Cayce and David Wilcock.

Wynn Free believes that not only is David Wilcock the reincarnation of Edgar Cayce, but that he also shares the same paranormal gifts that allowed the Sleeping Prophet to help others with health issues, give them information about their past lives, and share information about the future. [1] [2]

Edgar Cayce was called the Sleeping Prophet because he was able to put himself into some kind of self-induced sleep state by lying down on a couch, closing his eyes, and folding his hands over his stomach.

---

[1] http://www.coasttocoastam.com/guest/free-wynn/6364
[2] http://divinecosmos.com/

In experiencing a state of relaxation and meditation, this enabled him to place his mind in contact with all time and space, responding to a wide diversity of questions.

In reference to Reincarnation, documented evidence exists to say that personality traits, personal preferences, habits and behavior seem to carry over from one lifetime to another; so, too, do individuals bear a facial resemblance to whom they were before (refer to the work of both Dr. Michael Newton and Dr. Ian Stevenson).

The new bodies often have visible birthmarks in areas where the alleged self was wounded.

Does not this speak to the immortality of the human soul?

What I find so utterly fascinating is how closely young Edgar Cayce (photo on the left) also resembles young David Wilcock (photo on the right).

http://www.bbsradio.com/bbc/wynn_free/wynn_free.shtml

Negative karma weighs the soul down and hampers one's personal evolution.

It is the goal of every soul to enter into its next incarnation with as little negative karma as possible.

In essence, one lifetime is not enough to complete one's present evolutionary cycle; as a result, one reincarnates in a given epoch, until its evolutionary cycle has been mastered.

Chapter 1

Special Education teachers work with students who have a wide range of learning, mental, emotional and physical disabilities.

For students who have mild or moderate disabilities, they ensure that lessons and teaching strategies are modified to meet the needs of the student.

For students who have severe disabilities, they often focus on independent living skills, functional academics, career development and personal development. [3] [4]

---

[3]

http://www.ed.gov.nl.ca/edu/k12/studentsupportservices/publications/FunctionalCurriculumGuide.pdf

[4]

http://www.gnb.ca/0000/publications/ss/teachingstudentswithautismspectrumdisorders.pdf

Special education involves the education of students with special needs in a way that addresses both individual differences as well as needs.

In addition, special education is a term that is generally used to specifically indicate instruction of students whose special needs reduce their ability to learn independently within an ordinary classroom.

Ysabeau Gabrielle LeBlanc, a Special Education teacher for nine years, had always been employed in school settings whereby both inclusion and mainstreaming were employed as different approaches to teaching these mighty beings.

In an inclusive setting, students spend all, or at least more than half, of the school day with students who do not have special educational needs.

Given that inclusion *can* require substantial modification of the general curriculum, most schools may elect to use this approach for students with mild to moderate special needs; basically, a best teaching practices approach.

Students *might also* leave the regular classroom, on occasion, to attend smaller, more intensive instructional sessions in a resource room setting in order to receive other related services (such as speech and language therapy, occupational therapy and physical therapy).

By comparison, a mainstreamed setting tended to involve students with moderate to severe special needs; these students would be educated with non-disabled students during specific time periods, *based on their skills.*

These same mainstreamed students were often placed in separate classes exclusively for students with special needs, for the remainder of the school day

Ysabeau was quite familiar with Differentiated Instruction, wherein methodologies employed in a classroom must be varied to suit the individual needs of all children.

One can differentiate the content (topic), the process (activities), the product, and the environment, in the accommodating of different learning styles. [5] [6] [7] [8]

So, too, was she comfortable with the use of Assistive Technology, when warranted.

Her approach was always a four-fold one, regardless of whatever approach was employed; [1] no two children are alike, [2] no two children learn in the exact same way, [3] an enriched environment for one student is not necessarily an enriched environment for another, and [4] we should always teach children to think for themselves.

_____

[5]

http://members.shaw.ca/priscillatheroux/differentiating.html
[6]

http://members.shaw.ca/priscillatheroux/differentiatingstrategies.html
[7]

http://members.shaw.ca/priscillatheroux/differentiatinglinks.html
[8] http://members.shaw.ca/priscillatheroux/styles.html

She had delivered Alternate Courses (courses created to completely replace a prescribed course, generally offered within a resource room setting), Alternate Programs (intensive programs created to teach prerequisite skills and strategies, generally offered within a resource room setting) and Functional Programs (alternate curricula programming created to highlight independent living skills, functional academics, career development and personal development, generally offered within a segregated setting).

At thirty-two years of age, Ysabeau found herself moving to a new community, a new school; luckily, she had been given the name of a woman, Mrs. Llewelyn, who took in boarders.

Knowing that she would be turning thirty-three on her upcoming December 13th birthday, Ysabeau was eager to find herself stationed in a permanent school; one whereby she could establish herself within the community, married or not.

Chapter 2

Ghislain Navarre Clairmont, a sculptor and carpenter of twenty years, had spent the majority of his time working abroad, specializing in the Renaissance art form, the time period of several Quattrocento sculpturers; namely,

[1] Lorenzo Ghiberti (1378–1455) [9] [10] [11]

[2] Donato di Niccolò di Betto Bardi, known simply as Donatello (1386– 1466) [12] [13]

[3] Andrea del Verrocchio (1435–1488) [14] [15]

---

[9] http://www.visual-arts-cork.com/old-masters/lorenzo-ghiberti.htm

[10] http://simple.wikipedia.org/wiki/Goldsmith

[11] http://simple.wikipedia.org/wiki/Renaissance_art

[12] http://www.visual-arts-cork.com/old-masters/donatello.htm

[13] http://simple.wikipedia.org/wiki/Donatello

[14] http://www.visual-arts-cork.com/sculpture/andrea-del-verrocchio.htm

[15] http://simple.wikipedia.org/wiki/Andrea_del_Verrocchio

[4] Michelangelo di Lodovico Buonarroti Simoni, known simply as Michelangelo (1475–1564) [16] [17] [18] [19]

The transition period between the Medieval Era and the modern world, renaissance is a word that means *revival* or *rebirth.*

While the cultural center of the Renaissance was Italy, and in particular Florence, its influence stretched across Europe into both France as well as Germany; a time period of great achievements in both the arts as well as the sciences, combined with deep religious concerns, the Renaissance quickly became one of the most productive periods in history. [20]

---

[16] http://www.visual-arts-cork.com/old-masters/michelangelo-buonarroti.htm

[17] http://simple.wikipedia.org/wiki/Michelangelo

[18] http://simple.wikipedia.org/wiki/List_of_Renaissance_artists

[19] http://www.visual-arts-cork.com/history-of-art/quattrocento.htm

[20] http://www.yesnet.yk.ca/schools/projects/renaissance/index.shtml

There was a focus among Renaissance sculptors, as in ancient Greece, on portraying an idealized human form, often undertaken in the sculpting of nude male figures, especially biblical and mythical figures. [21]

Ghislain would often reference both Donatello's *David*, as well as Michelangelo's *David*, as being the most popular characteristic examples of this particular style.

As techniques advanced, copies (or casts) of small bronze nudes became rather popular; these were purchased by wealthy individuals as a means of decorating their homes. [22]

---

[21] http://www.ehow.com/info_8746404_characteristics-renaissance-sculptures.html#ixzz2Mi75KR5Y
[22] http://www.ehow.com/info_8746404_characteristics-renaissance-sculptures.html#ixzz2Mi75KR5Y

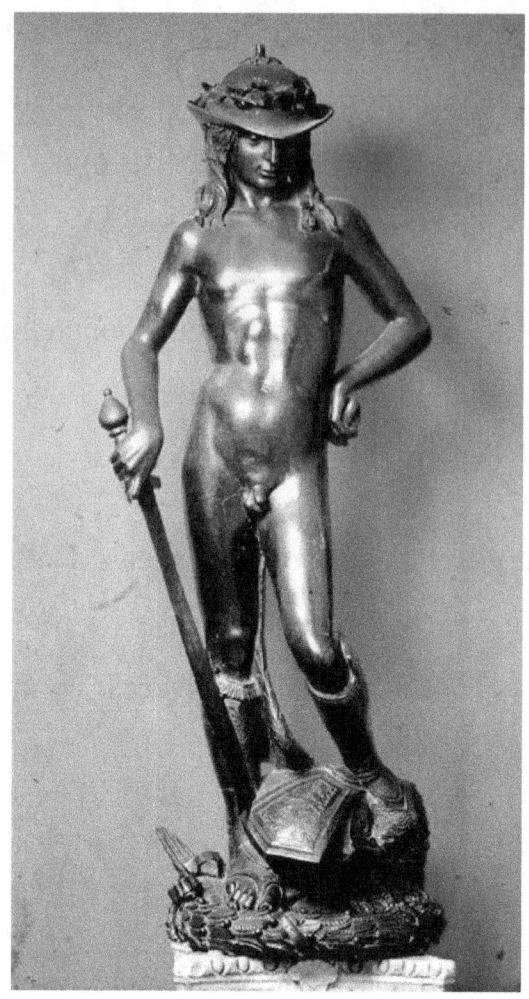

Bronze David by Donatello [23]

http://blogs.artinfo.com/secrethistoryofart/2011/02/15/inside
-the-masterpiece-verrocchios-david/

---

[23]

http://employees.oneonta.edu/farberas/arth/arth213/donatell
o_david.html

David by Michelangelo

http://en.wikipedia.org/wiki/File:Michelangelos_David.jpg

Used since the dawn of classical western sculpture, contrapposto (an Italian word that means counterpose) is a visual art technique that defines the realistic distribution of weight in a sculpture of a human. [24] [25]

As a result, contrapposto is denoted in the way a sculpted figure stands, with weight focused on one leg while the other is relaxed, thereby resulting in a realistic, curving shape as opposed to a more stiffly positioned posture. [26]

This concept, discovered in ancient Greece, was revived by the sculptors of the Renaissance.

---

[24]

http://employees.oneonta.edu/farberas/arth/arth213/donatello_david.html
[25] http://en.wikipedia.org/wiki/Contrapposto
[26] http://www.ehow.com/info_8746404_characteristics-renaissance-sculptures.html#ixzz2Mi75KR5Y

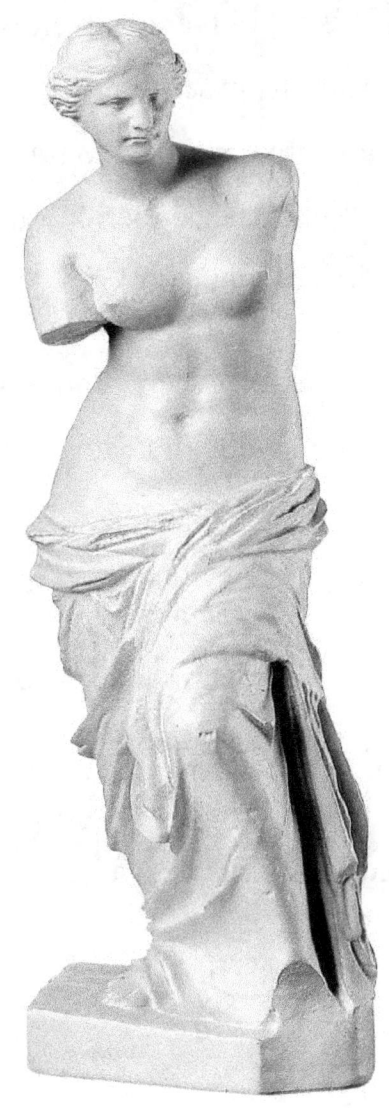

Venus de Milo by Alexandros

http://www.3dprint4ever.fr/wp-
content/uploads/2014/03/Venus-de-Milo.jpg

Precious metals, like gold and silver, were used less in sculpture than during the proceeding Gothic period, meaning that while the goldsmith continued to train some of the finest sculptors of the Renaissance period, their influence had become more limited to metalworking. [27]

This was the time period when bronze was given a more important role (employed first for reliefs, followed by statues or busts).[28]

Bronze was quick to become a most popular medium for the Renaissance sculptor, mainly because of its ductility (malleability) as well as its durability; so, too, was it popular because of its brilliance when gilded (coated with gold, gold leaf or a gold colored substance). [29]

---

[27] http://www.visual-arts-cork.com/sculpture/renaissance.htm#characteristics
[28] Ibid.
[29] Ibid.

The other bonus of sculpting in bronze was the ease with which pieces could be transported when compared to its counterpart in marble. [30]

Marble, Istrian stone (one of the most durable materials in Venetian architecture) and Pietra Serena (sandstone) were utilized for stone sculpture during the Renaissance period.

While wood was an inexpensive sculptural material, its use was generally limited to the thickly wooded regions of Europe.

Ghislain was partial to bronze sculpting, availing of the lost wax method of casting (known as *cire perdue*) which is a process that begins with the artist's original piece sculpted in clay, wood, stone or metal; this is the first step.

Even though the earliest records show the process to be over four thousand years old, the art bronzes of today are cast using the same ancient process. [31]

---

[30] http://library.thinkquest.org/23492/data/bronze.htm

Once the clay sculpture is completed, the entire process in the foundry takes anywhere from six weeks to four months to produce a single bronze. [32]

As a result, bronze sculptures are quite pricey.

The second step involves making a mold of the original sculpture by coating it with layers of silicone rubber, after which a plaster shell is made and fashioned over the hardened rubber.

This is the method that produces a rubber mold "in two easily-separated halves which can be pulled away from the artist's original [piece] without causing damage. The completed rubber mold, a *negative* version of the artist's *positive* original, becomes the new master from which all copies in an edition are made." [33]

The third step involves creating a wax duplicate of the artist's original sculpture.

---

[31] http://www.rosalindcook.com/clay-bronze-sculptures.htm
[32] http://www.rosalindcook.com/clay-bronze-sculptures.htm
[33] http://www.collectorsguide.com/fa/fa023.shtml

The interior of the rubber mold is first painted with molten wax.

Next, both halves of the mold are put together so that hot wax, in liquid form, can be "slushed" into the mold. [34]

As the wax cools, from the outside inward, to a thickness of ¼ inch, the excess wax is poured out, after which the rubber mold can be opened and the wax duplicate removed. [35]

The same process is utilized for every piece, so each mold must be carefully stored. This is the point whereby the artist usually spends hours, perhaps days, correcting any surface imperfections that may exist.

Step four involves adding a wax funnel to provide an entrance for the molten metal.

Wax rods (called sprues) are attached to the wax replica, a process that will prepare the piece for the bronze pour; so, too, do these channels create air vents, allowing trapped air

---

[34] http://www.collectorsguide.com/fa/fa023.shtml
[35] Ibid.

to be released when metal is poured into the mold, assuring an even flow throughout. [36]

Thereafter, the sprued wax figure is dipped into a ceramic solution before being rolled, or dipped, in fine sand (which gives detail), followed by a much coarser sand (which gives strength). [37]

This is repeated until the layers produce a strong ceramic mold about ¼ inch thick; the second *negative* in the process. [38]

Once hardened, the inverted ceramic mold is heated to 1800 degrees Farenheit; the wax melts and pours out of the ceramic shell (which is where the term lost wax, also known as *cire perdue*, comes from) and the mold is strengthened. [39]

This step normally takes between one and two weeks.

---

[36] http://www.collectorsguide.com/fa/fa023.shtml
[37] Ibid.
[38] Ibid.
[39] http://www.rosalindcook.com/clay-bronze-sculptures.htm

Step five involves the pouring of molten bronze, which is an alloy of copper, silicone and manganese, into the mold.

The empty ceramic shell is placed in a sand pit.

Molten bronze, heated to 2200 degrees Farenheit, is poured into the uppermost cup and down through the sprues into the cavities of the shell; as the bronze cools, the last *positive* is created. [40]

Refining this raw piece "is a delicate and demanding process that includes removing rods of bronze formed from the sprues, recreating the surface texture in these areas, and sandblasting remnants of the ceramic mold from the piece." [41]

In the case of any sculpture cast that requires more than one piece, the sections are assembled, through welding, at this time. Thereafter, the sculpture is then "ground to resemble the surface of the original sculpture.

---

[40] http://www.rosalindcook.com/clay-bronze-sculptures.htm
[41] http://www.collectorsguide.com/fa/fa023.shtml

This reworking of the surface is termed *metal chasing* and takes many hours of labor intensive work." [42]

The remaining step involves coloring the bronze.

The ancient Asians would bury their bronzes to naturally oxidize them, sometimes for years; today, however, the oxidation and coloring (called patina) takes place within hours. [43]

The patina is applied through brushing, or spraying, various chemicals onto the metal with or without heat; different chemicals are used to create a variety of colors. [44]

Interestingly, acrylic is often used to simulate chemical colors.

---

[42] http://www.rosalindcook.com/clay-bronze-sculptures.htm
[43] Ibid.
[44] Ibid.

Having settled in Lapland, Nova Scotia, a rural community situated 30 minutes from Bridgewater (the largest town in the South Shore region, with a population of 8,000, located at the mouth of the La Have River in Lunenburg County, with La Have having been the capital of Acadia from 1632 to 1635, during the time of Isaac de Razilly), 40 minutes from Mahone Bay (an area that was first settled during Father Le Loutre's War in 1749), and 50 minutes from Lunenburg (once an Acadian Mi'kmaq village named Mirligueche, also established under the direction of Isaac de Razilly), Ghislain was eager to finish building his home.

Soon to be turning forty-four on his upcoming December 13th birthday, he intuitively knew that this was where he was supposed to be; tired of the jet setting life, he was ready to put down roots whilst enjoying a more relaxed lifestyle.

For all of this to come to pass, however, so, too, was he also temporarily boarding with Mrs. Llewelyn, an *old* family friend.

Chapter 3

In the three months since becoming a boarder with Mrs. Elwen Llewelyn, Ghislain had never been present for meals when Ysabeau took hers.

Engaged in many supper conversations, Ysabeau came to learn that Elwen was a Welsh name that means *friend of the elves*.

So, too, did she come to understand that Llewelyn (an ancient Welsh name) was often used to reference Llewelyn the Great; a medieval Prince of Gwynedd, in north Wales, and eventually *de facto* ruler over most of Wales, it was through a combination of war and diplomacy that he dominated Wales for 40 years. [45]

Some sources stated that the name had been derived from the British names Lugobelinus and Cunobelinus, with others contending that it was derived from the Welsh *Llew* (which

---

[45] http://en.wikipedia.org/wiki/Llywelyn_the_Great

translates as Lion), from whence documents of the 15th century have shown the nickname Lleo. [46]

A lover of history, Ysabeau was intrigued to discover that Llewelyn had been born about 1173 (the son of Iorwerth ap Owain and the grandson of Owain Gwynedd, who had been ruler of Gwynedd until his death in 1170), probably at Dolwyddelan (although not in the present Dolwyddelan Castle, built by Llewelyn himself). [47] [48]

Llewelyn was also a descendant of the senior line of Rhodri Mawr, [49] making him a member of the princely house of Gwynedd. [50] [51]

[46] http://www.amethyst-night.com/names/welshsurs.html
[47] http://en.wikipedia.org/wiki/Llywelyn_the_Great
[48] http://en.wikipedia.org/wiki/File:Dolwyddelan_Castle,_Conwy,_Wales.jpg
[49] http://en.wikipedia.org/wiki/Rhodri_Mawr
[50] http://en.wikipedia.org/wiki/Llywelyn_the_Great
[51] http://en.wikipedia.org/wiki/Kingdom_of_Gwynedd

Llywelyn's mother, Marared (a name that was occasionally anglicized to Margaret) was the daughter of Madog ap Maredudd, Prince of Powys. [52] [53] [54]

Elwen had married her college sweetheart, Dafydd Llewelyn, moving from her home in the Preseli Mountain area in north Pembrokeshire, West Wales, famed for the Preseli Bluestone of Stonehenge, to Bridgewater, Nova Scotia, in 1972.

It was here that they had raised their family.

Meeting Ghislain, over the Christmas holidays, Ysabeau felt an instant rapport and comfort level that she seldom experienced. An immediate sense of déjà vu, it seemed as if they had known each other before; old souls, if you will.

---

[52] http://en.wikipedia.org/wiki/Llywelyn_the_Great
[53] http://en.wikipedia.org/wiki/Madog_ap_Maredudd
[54] http://en.wikipedia.org/wiki/Kingdom_of_Powys

"My mother's favorite movie was the fantasy film, Ladyhawke; hence, my name, Isabeau, but with the Y spelling variant. Ysabeau is Medieval French, an ancient form of Isabelle."

"The title of the movie sounds intriguing."

"It is actually. The movie is about two lovers, Isabeau and Navarre, who are doomed to lifelong separation by a demonic curse invoked by the corrupt and jealous Bishop of Aquila.

"By day, Isabeau is transformed into a hawk; at night, Navarre becomes a wolf. It is only at dusk and dawn of each day that they are able to see each other in human form for one fleeting moment, but never touching.

"Imperius, the monk who originally betrayed them, finds a way to break the curse, but only if he and Mouse, a thief facing execution who escapes the dungeons of Aquila by way of the sewers, whose real name is Philippe Gaston, can get them back into Aquila to face the Bishop."

Before continuing, Ysabeau allowed herself a reminiscent smile.

"A lover of history, so, too, did my mother become fascinated with Henri III, King of Navarre, the first monarch of the Bourbon branch of the Capetian dynasty, and his mistress, Gabrielle d'Estrées; hence, my middle name. Henry III became Henry IV of France, and thereafter the crown of Navarre passed to the kings of France."

Ghislain smiled an encouraging smile, even though he was not yet ready to let Ysabeau know that his middle name was Navarre, for fear that the synchronicity would frighten her.

"It appears that this love of history has also been passed along to you."

Ghislain surprised Ysabeau one fine spring Saturday morning.

"You know that I'm building a house in Lapland. I would love for you to see it. Would you be interested in taking a little trip with me?"

Ysabeau beamed.

"Mrs. Llewelyn has told me that you are extremely gifted with your hands, both as a sculptor as well as a carpenter. I would *love* to see what has been taking all of your time. Thank you for asking me."

Ghislain smiled.

"I have to run out to get a few things. Why don't we meet, in the main foyer, say, in about half an hour?"

"That sounds perfect!"

Ysabeau was immediately taken with the design of the house; an ornate romantic stone Gothic Revival Victorian home, highlighting all of the tracery and ornamentation, found on a stone Gothic cathedral, but imitated in flat scroll-cut wood, complete with latticed widows and an upper balcony window, nestled within an evergreen forest.

On the large rural lot, this home took on both the grandeur of a stone castle, as well as the comforts of a farmhouse with a dressed-up exterior.

In admiring the look of the home, Ysabeau felt as if she had been transported to another time, another place.

Tears filled her eyes and she hastily wiped them away.

"This is so very beautiful, Ghislain. How have you managed to accomplish this on your own?"

"With much patience, much fortitude and much tenderness," came the immediate reply; a reply that almost sounded like an encrypted message.

Ysabeau always felt that no style of Victorian interior decorating was more romantic than Gothic Revival.

She knew Gothic revival home decor to be a style that both celebrated, and idealized, the Middle Ages, embodying the romantic tales of knights and dragons, of King Arthur, Gwenevere, and Lancelot, of mythical gargoyles and unicorns; so, too, were they representative of the ecclesiastical architecture of Europe's grand cathedrals like Chartres, Notre Dame, and Westminster Abbey. [55]

The Victorian Gothic Revival of the 19th century was a far more sumptuous style than the original Gothic period of the Middle Ages.

---

[55] http://www.squidoo.com/gothic-revival-victorian-home-decor

Most homes of the Medieval era were sparsely and plainly furnished, but that did not appeal to Victorian sensibilities, thus they drew inspiration, instead, from the wealthy who built, and furnished, ornate castles and cathedrals. [56]

The Gothic Revival Victorian style features elaborated tracery in wood and stone, dark wood paneling, carved statuary, stained, leaded glass windows, heraldic imagery, ribbed vaulted ceilings, and pointed arches borrowed from the Middle Ages; this was a style that Ysabeau had always felt at home with. [57]

As well, the extraordinary tapestries, and other types of needlework, whilst hung primarily on the walls, had also served as draperies and table coverings. [58]

---

[56] http://www.squidoo.com/gothic-revival-victorian-home-decor
[57] Ibid.
[58] Ibid.

Gothic Revival fabrics, rich and substantial, had been woven from wool, flax, linen and other natural fibers that were made into draperies for beds, walls and windows, to keep out the drafts. [59]

With faux painted dark walnut beamed ceilings being the chief focal point of the lower level rooms, the house took on a dated look from a time long past.

The main floor showcased an open layout in which the family room, kitchen, and dining room were all open to one another; a feature that seemed to flow effortlessly, with great beauty.

The family room was host to an ornate Windsor Arch Front radiant gas fireplace, [60] complete with mantel, handcrafted in Sienna marble; the focal point of the room.

---

[59] http://www.squidoo.com/gothic-revival-victorian-home-decor

[60] http://www.valorfireplaces.com/products/portrait_windsor.php

In the kitchen, the AGA Total Control Range Cooker, [61] a cast iron baking, roasting and slow cooking oven (with boiling and simmering hotplates, large enough to accommodate several large stockpots and multiple pans), pewter in color, was clearly the pièce de résistance, serving to create a timeless look.

A free standing island, fashioned after the large work tables found in many historic kitchen homes (but not to be used for sitting and eating at), also gave the impression of perpetuity.

An avid reader and researcher by nature, Ysabeau's favorite room was the huge Library, on the main level at the back, complete with stained glass header above the entryway and large lattice windows overlooking the forest.

Complete with custom built wall to wall, richly carved, rosewood bookcases that filled the entire back wall, the upper shelves needed to be reached by a sturdy ladder on wheels.

---

[61] http://www.aga-ranges.com/products/aga-total-control.aspx

With a fireplace, also identical to that located in the main family area, situated in one corner of the room, and a computer area in the other, the space appeared to be a necessary merger between past and present, evoking a space of timeless beauty; a subtle hint of distinction and elegance from a time once forgotten.

While Ghislain was still working on the upper level, the vaulted and beamed ceiling of the Master Suite was its most magnificent feature.

Complete with a separate living space, designer Tessa Kennedy's dramatic Gothic Revival bed, [62] an expansive walk-in closet, complete with fireplace and spacious double sink master bathroom enclave, Ysabeau had never before been privy to such elegance.

There were five additional rooms on the upper level, only one of which was totally completed.

---

[62]

http://www.abbeville.com/interiors.asp?ISBN=1558597999 &CaptionNumber=02

Ghislain explained that he would gladly show her the finished room, one that he always kept locked, but only when he felt it appropriate to do so.

What mystery was he harboring within this sacred space?

Chapter 4

It was fate that had brought Ysabeau back into Ghislain's life.

Knowing that he was not allowed to assist in any way, all Ghislain could do was invite Ysabeau, for regular visits; she had to come to remember things on her own.

The more time Ysabeau spent within Ghislain's home, furnished with various pieces of sculpture, that seemed haunting familiar to her, the more she was coming to believe that they had shared a past life.

How else could she explain the sunshine, within her heart, that felt close to bursting, but only when they were together?

Chapter 5

Summer vacation had finally arrived and Ysabeau was finding that she was spending more and more time with Ghislain; a work apprentice of sorts.

One day, whilst on her own, she found the special room to be unlocked; suffice it to say curiosity far outweighed waiting for Ghislain to take her on a tour of the finished room.

She entered to discover a shrine to eternal love, complete with clothing items, genuine jewelry pieces, books and rare manuscripts, all of which spoke to different eras in time.

In her intimate perusal, she chanced across the most exquisite looking band encrusted with jewels, experiencing immediate déjà vu.

The memory, so close, as was demonstrated by the abrasive, persistent, third eye headache, continued to remain elusive.

Ghislain returned to find Ysabeau in the sanctuary; they continued to stare at each other in the distance; she began to sob, deep heart wrenching sobs.

Leading her to the window seat for two, where they remained for the longest time, Ghislain could only hold her, stroking her hair, while she cried.

Adamant that everything had to do with the ring, locked behind a glass case, Ghislain asked her if she wanted to hold the piece; she nodded in the affirmative.

Placing the ring in the palm of her hand, what she experienced next defied human comprehension.

She remembered that they were both immortal at one time, becoming mortal by choice.

So, too, did she come to understand that born into each lifetime, with memories completely intact, Ghislain had always continued to search for her, his twin soul.

Chapter 6

Ancient Lemuria

While it has been stated that theories of modern tectonics, currently accepted by the larger scientific community, appear to have rendered the concept of Lemuria obsolete, we *know* Lemuria to have existed.

How is it that we can state this with such authority, you ask?

We know because we lived during this time.

This was the beginning of choice for us.

We, alone, decided, as immortal beings, that we wanted, in addition to our spiritual gifts of clairvoyance, clairaudience and telepathy, to experience a human existence.

We wanted to feel.

We wanted to touch.

We wanted to taste.

We wanted to smell.

We became the core race of the planet Earth, the first of the so-called humans, older than the Sumerians, older than those from the Indus Valley, receiving our seed biology from the stars, courtesy of the Pleiadians, about 100,000 years ago.

The story of creation, as told in the Bible, comes close to the metaphysical view of what happened after receiving our two new awareness DNA layers: we began to act out the process of duality, the awareness of light and dark.

Earth, then, became the *only planet of free choice* of its time.

Angels began the process of coming to the planet, using the human body as the vehicle to create this test of Earth; it was at this time, about 50,000 years ago, that humans began to demonstrate true enlightened humanity.

We, the Lemurians, were a full-fledged, mature civilization from 35,000 years ago to about 15,000 years ago.

Possessing quantum consciousness, our sense of time was far different; we existed in, what would today have been considered, a timeless state of being.

In truth, Lemuria was the grandest society this planet has ever seen; not huge in numbers, but in both consciousness as well as quantum awareness, living in peace for more than 20,000 years.

Having lived successfully for more than 20,000 years around the base of the island you call Hawaii, the Lemurians were aware they lived in a basin (a valley) that was lower than the average water level of the earth.

With the main seas held back by some of the mountain ranges that existed before the shifting of plate tectonics, we knew we were vulnerable to the water level of the planet, should it rise; as long as it stayed cool, we were fine.

We also knew that we lived in the shadow of the hot spot, a large tectonic plate, a plate that could move once again, as it had before.

In addition to being drawn to the energy of volcanism, the islands we worshiped upon were all active volcanoes.

The ice started melting 15,000 years ago; by this time the Lemurians had become a sea-faring society. Knowing what was eventually going to happen, we had become interested in ships.

From 15,000 years ago to 10,000 years ago, the water balance of the earth changed, pouring into the valleys of Lemuria.

Some of the Lemurians stayed on the mountain, climbing as the waters about them continued to rise. In fact, the top of the Lemurian capital mountain is now a series of islands called Hawaii; today you would refer to their ancestors as the Polynesians.

Others began other societies in combination with humans who had traveled far from the core, and had forgotten their lineage completely.

One of the earliest cultures, the culture of the Sumerian people, was situated in the Middle East.

Eventually, this led to the Egyptian culture many years later.

While the ancient Sumerians did not have telescopes, they knew all about the cosmos; their inter-dimensional sight gave them this intuitive perception to *know* what was around them.

As Lemurians, so, too, did we have this same ability, albeit stronger, given our inter-dimensional DNA.

We were here long enough for our language, the Solara Maru, to evolve and change, providing the seeds for some of the most profound languages that you know today; indeed, the Solara Maru became the root language for several of your sacred languages, including Sanskrit and Hebrew.

Over time, we experienced a *devolution* (the opposite of evolution) in that we began to lose certain abilities.

As old souls, older than recorded history, we were part of an experience that we remember; an experience that still surges through our DNA.

OUR MESSAGE TO YOU IN YOUR TIME

As humans, you create your own future, you create your own prophecy.

All are now on a completely different track; one that was not foreseen by prophets of ages past.

Less than one-half of one percent of this planet has to awaken in order to make a difference in the vibration for all; you have already moved into 2012 with a new vibration.

We ask that you let go of all your old, and outmoded, patterns; we ask that you let go of anything that has been shared with in order to build a world that is fake.

We ask that you open yourself to new thoughts and explanations.

As you are growing a new planet consciousness, many are claiming that your DNA is being activated; some are even referring to this as ascension.

To put it simply, you are returning to the Lemuria-like state.

We are all one, the children of God/dess, the Creator of All that is.

Chapter 7

Ancient Egypt

Armana Dynasty

I am she, the one history has come to know as Nefertiti; an Egyptian name that means *the beautiful one who has come.*

I was both co-regent and Great Wife of Pharaoh Akhenaten, the tenth King of the 18th Dynasty; the man history now refers to as the Heretic king.

History tells you that under Akhenaten's father, Egypt was the strongest, and wealthiest, nation in the world, covering territory from as far north as Syria to as far south as Sudan; indeed, this is true.

My husband was a revolutionary, most notably made famous for his religious reforms.

Whilst he attempted to supplant the complex polytheism religion of Egypt (a pantheon of gods and goddesses) with a more monotheist centered approach around the Aten (the radiant sun disk), it needs to be stated that the Egyptian religion did not actually become monotheistic, for cults related to the other gods and goddesses continued to persist; in truth, they were never erased from Egyptian theology.

We knew the Aten to be a single entity, the life giving force. Whilst not actually worshipping the visible sun-disk that could be seen traversing the sky each day (a three-dimensional spherical globe you know to be the sun), we were using the sun-disk as a symbol of a single God.

Our artistic representation of the Aten became that of a sun disk, reaching down with rays of light in the form of hands to touch (and embrace) our family.

http://upload.wikimedia.org/wikipedia/commons/e/e4/Aten_
disk.jpg

Much like the sun, the visible entity that was recognized as the generative, and restorative, power of the universe, we knew the power of a single God to be the same; all of nature was a work of the creator and it was therefore intrinsically good.

As alluded to earlier, we viewed the sun disk as being the iconic representation of the cosmic creator; the one and only God that represented radiating light, balance and beauty.

With my husband having assumed the role of High Priest of the Aten, I was accorded a degree of prominence that no other major civilization in the ancient world was willing to concede to a woman.

Indeed, we were the first triad; a triad consisting of the Aten, my husband and myself. In this capacity, we were representative of both male and female, the totality of all creation.

In offering adoration to the rising sun each morning, we no longer had need of any intermediary; no more priests, no more oracles, no more magic, no more processions, and no need for statues, since the sun was visible to all.

The new religion was a system that was immutable; only the king was able to define it.

Priests lost most of their power; the concept of Divine Kingship was further emphasized with Akhenaten being the sole representative of Aten on earth.

As servants of God maintaining the domain of the Aten, our offering had become a sign of recognition for his goodness; nothing was expected in return.

Why, then, did my husband feel a need for such a religious revolution?

Akhenaton feared that the wealth, power and prestige of the Amen priesthood might lead to the rise of a parallel government, one that would threaten his monarchy; so, too, were we motivated by our shared belief in a single God, a single entity, therefore endeavoring to turn our belief system into the official religion of Egypt.

It also needs to be shared that both Akhenaten's father (Amenhotep III) and grandfather (Thutmose IV) also venerated the sun god Aten; just not to the same degree as ourselves.

Although my husband did not change everything, as has so often been stated, he was successful in causing an upheaval of great significance, forever branding him a revolutionary.

If we were to further define Atenism (the name that has been given to our natural philosophy of life), we would state the following: [1] Atenism is a belief in the creator of all life, meaning an ethereal consciousness that dwells on a higher plane than that of humanity, [2] Each individual represents a facet of the Aten, and [3] Each individual represents the power of the One.

In fact, the main reason for depicting Aten with the royal family was to reinforce our divinity (as well as your own); it was never to serve any so-called magical purpose.

Chapter 8

The Merovingian Dynasty

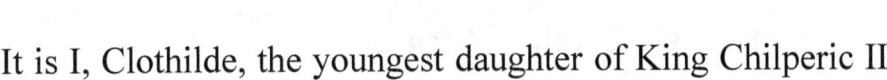

It is I, Clothilde, the youngest daughter of King Chilperic II of Burgundy, granddaughter of Gundioc, King of Burgundy.

My grandfather ruled the areas of Saône, Dauphiny, Savoie and a part of Provence, setting up Vienne as the capital of the kingdom of Burgundy; when he died, his territory was divided amongst four sons.

In all, there were eight Burgundian kings (of the house of Gundahar) who ruled until the kingdom was overrun by the Franks in 534 AD.

My father succeeded his father in 473 AD as King of Burgundy at Lyon.

I was born, in 475 AD, at the Burgundian court of Lyon.

Following the murder of my parents (493 AD), my eldest sister and I were driven into exile by our paternal uncle, King Gundobad.

We were immediately taken into custodial protection by his brother, King Godegesil, in Vienne.

Having been seen by the envoys of Clovis I, King of the Franks, they told their master of my beauty and intelligence. Not long thereafter, Clovis requested my hand in marriage; shortly after the formal bethrothal, I become his second wife.

Clovis and Godegisel were quick to ally against Gundobad in a long, drawn out civil war.

Having succeeded his father, Childeric I, a Merovingian king of the Salian Franks, in 481 AD at the age of fifteen, he did not know Catholicism.

A strong and determined woman, active in determining my own destiny, I would not rest until he had completely renounced Arianism, thereby embracing the Catholic faith.

We had been married for close to three years before he finally converted. Baptized on Christmas Day in 496 AD, in a small church in the vicinity of the subsequent Abbey of Saint-Remi in Reims (a UNESCO World Heritage Site in your time), he was quick to leave behind the Arian heresy that many other Germanic peoples continued to subscribe to.

The Frankish kingdom, thereafter, was solidified as a Catholic nation; an alliance with the papacy had been created.

Following the death of my husband in 511 AD, I retired to the Abbey of Saint-Martin in Tours (built in the Middle Ages, but thoroughly demolished during the French Revolution of your time). For all who look for me, you will find me buried beside Clovis in the Church of the Holy Apostles; the one we co-founded in Paris (today called the Abbey of Sainte-Geneviève).

A sculpture of Saint Clotilde, Notre-Dame de Corbeil, 12th century

http://en.wikipedia.org/wiki/File:Sainte_Clotilde.JPG

Saint Clotilde

http://commons.wikimedia.org/wiki/File:Vitrail_Florac_010
609_12.jpg

Clovis statue at the Abbey Church of Saint-Denis

http://upload.wikimedia.org/wikipedia/commons/0/0e/Sculpt
ure.Notre.Dame.de.Corbeil.png

Chapter 9

Kingdom of Camelot

574 AD

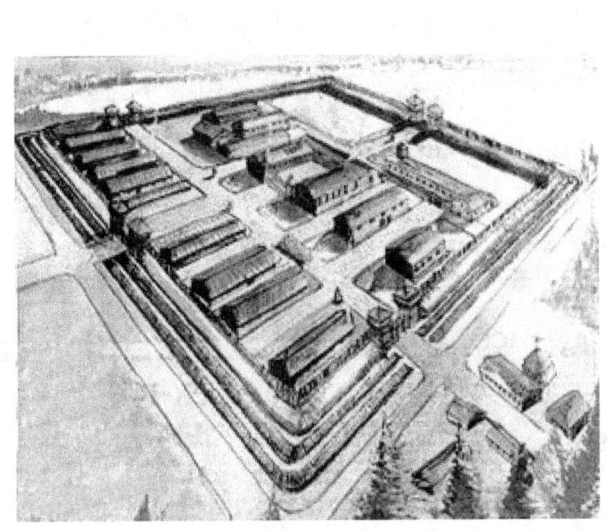

The Kingdom of Manann (Manau)

Roman Fortress (Ad Vallum) of Colonia at Camelon

http://www.britannia.com/history/arthur/camelon.html

The land between the two Roman Walls (the Antonine Wall in the North, running between the river Forth and the river Clyde, and Hadrians Wall in the South, running between the river Tyne and the Solway Firth) was a domain separate from the rest of Britain; a land split into many tiny kingdoms.

My name is Gwenevere. I married Prince Arturius (Artúr), eldest son of King Áedán mac Gabráin, in 574 AD; the same year that Saint Columba chose Áedán mac Gabráin, an experienced ruler, to become the Chief King of the Scots of Dál Riata (a Gaelic kingdom on the western coast of Scotland), the most powerful king of the North.

There has been much written about my husband that is complete falsehood; whilst a formidable Celtic Warrior, he was *never* King.

The tiny kingdom of Manann (Manau), situated on the east coast of Scotland, also belonged to King Áedán mac Gabráin; it was here that he had ruled, in 570 AD, before becoming the Chief King of the Scots of Dál Riata.

Situated where the old Roman Fortress (Ad Vallum) had been built, on the sloping land above the River Carron at Camelon, so, too, was the kingdom of Manann often referred to as Camelot.

The Pictish tribe, known as the Maetae or Miathi, lived immediately north of Manann.

Given Manann's close proximity to both the Picts and the Saxons, there were many skirmishes and battles that took place in this area.

Unable to maintain control over both kingdoms, Áedán mac Gabráin needed an able leader (commander, warrior, general) to fight for him in his absence, maintaining the borders of the kingdom; he chose Arturius (Artúr).

It was Saint Columba who accurately predicted that Áedán's younger son, Eochaid Buide, would succeed him instead of his chosen sons.

So, too did he predict the deaths of Arturius (Artúr), Eochaid Find, and Domangart, while fighting battles for their father.

Indeed, it was just as he had predicated; my husband Arturius (Artúr) was slain in the Battle of Miathi in 582 AD; we were married but eight years.

This was a battle fought against the Maeatae (a tribe of Picts who inhabited the land adjacent to Áedán's kingdom of Manann) near the River Forth in Manau. [63]

The Britons had a different name for this battle, calling it the Battle of Camallan.

---

[63] http://www.kingarthurlegend.com/kingdom-of-manann.html

Despite Áedán's victory, this was a very costly battle; a total of three hundred and three men were killed, numbers that included two sons: Arturius (Artúr) and Eochaid Find.

After the death of my husband, I was abducted, and taken further North, by the Picts; the very opponents of Arturius (Artúr).

Shortly after I was taken, I died and was buried at a place called Meigle (the extreme eastern borders of Perthshire), the heartland of Pictish territory.

In an earlier twist to this story, there was a battle fought between rival British kingdoms:

[1] the Christian British, which included King Ryderrch of Dumbarton, King Urien of Rheged (Gore) and King Áedán mac Gabráin.

[2] the Pagan British, which included the druid Myrddin (Merlin) and Gwenddlau, the Pagan Prince.

This battle was known as the Battle of Arderydd (573 AD).

The Christians were the victors.

After the Battle of Arderydd, Myrddin wandered, alone, in the forest of Celyddon, hunted by his enemies, which included King Ryderrch; many years later, however, King Ryderrch invited Myrddin to leave the forest, coming under his protection.

Chapter 10

Cathars at Montségur

March 16, 1244

My earthly name was Ermengarde d'Ussat. As a believer, I found my way to Montségur, where I was welcomed in 1240.

Known by the enemy as the Cathari, or Pure Ones, our lives were simple; we esteemed peace, harmony, love and tolerance for other belief systems.

Though many have referred to our belief system as a Christian heresy, in truth, ours was a completely different religion.

Finding it most difficult to understand how our God, one that is all powerful, merciful and good, could allow such monstrous evil to exist in this world, we knew there to be two eternal principles that divided the universe.

The good principle created the world of the spirits, and the evil principle created the material world. As living beings standing at the juncture of both; we were fallen spirits imprisoned in temporal, physical, bodies.

The goal of spiritual life, then, was to seek complete liberation from the material world through spiritual purification.

As believers in the transmigration of souls (reincarnation), we were aware that new beings had to be brought to Earth in order to accommodate the souls of the people who had not yet reached the required spiritual state, at their death, to go to heaven.

So, too, did this mean that we would come back, in successive reincarnations, in order to complete this arduous task of achieving gnosis.

Whilst we rejected the Old Testament with its vengeful and angry God (because this was the very God who created the physical world), we espoused the Ten Commandments.

In keeping, we also held fast to the following ......

[1] We would never submit to the telling of a falsehood; in fact, we preferred to say nothing at all rather than to lie.

[2] We refused to swear obedience to any being, knight, vassal, Baron or otherwise, as this could lead to much conflict between said obligations (coming from one's actions) and rules (based on our faith).

[3] We refused to swear before God as this would mean involving Him in all things of a material nature and this was against our faith.

[4] Having reached a high spiritual level, if one were to become a *perfect*, this meant that he or she must promise to totally renounce the evil of the material world in all ways; this included both dietary restrictions and total abstinence from sexual relations.

[5] As a *perfect*, we promised not to kill animals or eat the meat of a slain animal because we knew that a man could be reincarnated as an animal; so, too, could an animal reincarnate as a man. Whilst fish was permitted, we did not eat of any animal based foods.

[6] Living a life of prayer and contemplation was necessary to be able to access the wisdom of the inner self.

In reciting the Patter (our only prayer) [64] twice, not only were we able to concentrate on the meaning behind the words, but we were also attempting to enter into a closer communication with the Divine.

> Our father, which art in Heaven,
> Hallowed be thy name.
> Thy kingdom come,
> Thy will be done on Earth as it is in Heaven.
> Give us this day our supplementary bread,
> And remit our debts as we forgive our debtors.
>
> And keep us from temptation and free us from evil.
> Thine is the kingdom, the power and glory forever and ever.
> Amen.

[7] The *perfecti* always traveled, and ate with, a companion; a way to reduce the effects of temptation so as not to fall into sin.

[8] We promised never to betray the faith, even under the threat of death (be that by water or by fire).

---

[64] http://www.gnostique.net/documents/Cathar_Pater.pdf

[9] In refusing to fight, so, too, did we promise never to kill; only in very special and dangerous circumstances did we accept the *Endura* (a practice whereby one would stop eating and simply fast unto their death). [65]

[10] We held fast to but one sacrament, the *Consolamentum*; while it could be administered anywhere, it was generally reserved for use in cases of danger or urgency.

Uncomfortable with titles of any sort, we simply called ourselves *Les Bons Hommes* (Good Men), *Les Bonnes Femmes* (Good Women) and *Les Bons Chrétiens* (Good Christians). [66]

There existed a stark contrast between our teachings and the arrogance displayed by Rome.

---

[65] http://www.cathar.info/12011005_endura.htm

[66] http://gnosis.org/library/cathar-two-principles.htm

We knew the Roman Church to be the deliverer of a message of vast material wealth, lust, power and corruption; instead, we chose to embrace the Apostolic ideal as displayed by Christ.

We wanted nothing more than to be able to separate from Rome in order to band together in a life of purity and devotion to God; ours was a more brotherly, egalitarian society, freed from the heavy hierarchy of the Roman Church.

We held no lavish church properties; all of our services were held in homes or outside in the fields and forests.

As an authentic and responsible Christian, I was called upon to share the love of God with another; in doing so, my heart and mind were also renewed.

As Cathari, we merely sought to reach out to the world with love and friendship.

As a *credent*, a believer, a follower, I was not expected to adopt the austere lifestyle of the *perfect*, who, in living lives of extreme poverty, also abstained from sexual contact and eating meat. It was the *perfecti* who functioned as priests, but in a manner much more restrictive than that of Rome.

Like the Gnostics who came before us, we accorded Mary Magdalene significant importance; in fact, it was her vital role as a teacher that contributed to our belief that women could also serve as spiritual leaders.

We also knew her to be the wife of Jesus (Yeshua).

The majority of the women who became *perfecti* did so upon receiving the *consolamentum* after having been widowed; a position of far more prestige than anything offered through Rome.

Whilst still being able to maintain their own houses, these women, like their male counterparts, were also required to adhere to a strict and ascetic lifestyle.

While few of our female *perfecti* traveled to preach the faith, they still played a vital role in the spreading of our faith by establishing group homes for women. It was here that other women were educated in the faith; in bearing their own children, so, too, would they also become believers.

As each successive generation passed, the Cathar faith grew exponentially.

Our beliefs and practices were firmly founded on the Gospel of John. [67]

As the supreme teacher, we knew that Jesus (Yeshua) came to reveal, not to redeem; we also acknowledged all of the great teachers of the ages who had shown the truth of Love.

---

[67] http://gnosis.org/library/Interrogatio_Johannis.html

As a Church of Love (Amor), we believed in the liberation, and promotion, of individual strength. So, too, were we the keepers of the <u>Book of Love</u>, a secret gospel of Jesus (Yeshua), written not in words, but in symbols derived from a very ancient tradition; a book that was given to John the Divine

Like Jesus (Yeshua), the *perfecti* lived the simple life; one that involved teaching, caring, preaching and healing. The healing they practiced was two-fold: one based on medicinal plants and herbs, the other based on spiritual means.

On the last night of the siege of Montségur, the last major Cathar stronghold to resist the Crusaders, *perfecti* present gave the *credentes* the option to become *perfecti* (which meant that they would also be condemned to the stake) or to go free as part of the conditions of surrender. .

I was one of the twenty six *credentes* who eagerly came forward.

So, too, did Raimond de Niort, Seigneur of Usson, come forward; a crossbowman, he had arrived at Montségur between May and June of 1243.

Married to Marquesia, the daughter of Pierre-Roger de Mirepoix, Raimond had managed a small castle, near the village of Usson-les-Bains above the valley of the Aude, towards the south of the Cathar region; a lonely place, the castle stood out starkly against the unusually deep blue sky.

Upon our meeting, we knew that we had been together in many past lives.

Approaching impending death, I made ready to receive the *Consolamentum* (a sacrament unique to the Cathars) in the early hours of March 16, 1244, from Rixende de Telle, Mother superior of the *perfectae* at Montségur during the siege.

We marched down the southern slopes of the pog, positioning ourselves on a mass execution pyre of wood and logs that had been prepared earlier at the foot of the hill.

Some climbed ladders to the top of the bier; others entered into an enclosure and were tied to stakes positioned in the wood.

After reciting the Patter, the pyre was set on fire.

Chapter 11

House of Bourbon

1591

Christened as Gabrielle d'Estrées in 1573, daughter of Antoine III d'Estrées and Françoise Babou de La Bourdaisière, [68] my earliest days were spent at the fortified Château de Coeuvres-et-Valsery. [69]

In his younger days, my father, Antoine IV d'Estrées, a tall handsome man of noble bearing and high courage, was heir to a family of ancient lineage in Picardy.[70]

68

http://gw.geneanet.org/genroy?lang=fr;p=antoine+iv;n=d+estrees

[69] https://www.flickr.com/photos/biron-philippe/7409987912/in/photostream/

[70] http://books.google.ca/books?id=z8o1AQAAMAAJ&pg=P

My grandfather, Jean I d'Estrées (Seigneur d'Estrées, Seigneur de Valiers, Seigneur de Coeuvres, Seigneur de Viérey, Comte d'Orbec, Baron de Doudeauville and Vis-comte de Soissons) was born into an aristocratic and military family, at Coeuvres-et Valsery in 1486.

I now wish to present, to you, my paternal lineage.

[1] Pierre d'Estrées, dit Carbonnel, Seigneur de Boulant, Seigneur de Hamel, Seigneur d'Istres and Seigneur de l'Enclos-Maury, married Marie de Beaumont (daughter of Jean de Beaumont, Seigneur de Neuvirel (close to Corbie), amd Marie de La Houssaye); they had one son and two daughters. [71] [72] [73]

A221&lpg=PA221&dq=chateau+de+coeuvres+%2B+Antoi
ne+d%E2%80%99Estr%C3%A9es&source=bl&ots=Fwnwf
UMAS3&sig=CUMcyzecv3-
iGoI1WgwIGtrArh0&hl=en&sa=X&ei=juBLU7eWKsee2g
Xek4G4Dg&ved=0CFcQ6AEwDQ#v=onepage&q=chateau
%20de%20coeuvres%20%2B%20Antoine%20d%E2%80%
99Estr%C3%A9es&f=false

[71] Les d'Estrées: leurs domains et leurs liens de parenté au pays de Bray (Haute-Normandie): Notes généalogiques et historiques oar un Neufchatellois (page 7).

[72] http://racineshistoire.free.fr/LGN/PDF/Estrees.pdf (pg 2)

[2] Antoine I d'Estrées, Seigneur de Boulant and Seigneur de Valieu en Santerre, married Jeanne d'Aix (daughter of Hélie, Seigneur d'Aiz (or Aise, Aize, in the county of Saint-Pol) and Péronne de Noyelles) on September 12, 1447; they had three sons. [74] [75] [76]

[3] Antoine d'Estrées, dit le Jeune, Seigneur de Valieu, married Jeanne, Dame de la Cauchie, Dame de Neuville, Dame de Locquin and Dame de Watteland en Boulonnais (daughter of Guillaume, Seigneur de la Cauchie, Seigneur de Neuville, Seigneur de Wissant and Seigneur de Locquin and

---

[73] François-Alexandre Aubert de la Chesnaye des Bois (1773). Dictionnaire de la noblesse, contenant les généalogies, l'histoire et la chronologie des familles nobles de France (page 194).

[74] http://racineshistoire.free.fr/LGN/PDF/Estrees.pdf (pg 2)

[75] Les d'Estrées: leurs domains et leurs liens de parenté au pays de Bray (Haute-Normandie): Notes généalogiques et historiques oar un Neufchatellois (page 9).

[76] François-Alexandre Aubert de la Chesnaye des Bois (1773). Dictionnaire de la noblesse, contenant les généalogies, l'histoire et la chronologie des familles nobles de France (page 195).

Jeanne de Licques); they had two sons and two daughters. [77]
[78]

La Cauchie was a hamlet of the village of Locquin, five miles from Calais.

In 1500, Antoine d'Estrées, dit le Jeune, was a Gentleman of the King's House (King Louis XII). [79]

[4] Jean I d'Estrées, the eldest of the four children, was born in 1486; he died on October 23, 1567. [80] [81] [82]

---

[77] Les d'Estrées: leurs domains et leurs liens de parenté au pays de Bray (Haute-Normandie): Notes généalogiques et historiques oar un Neufchatellois (pages 9 and 10).
[78] http://racineshistoire.free.fr/LGN/PDF/Estrees.pdf (pg 2)
[79] François-Alexandre Aubert de la Chesnaye des Bois (1773). Dictionnaire de la noblesse, contenant les généalogies, l'histoire et la chronologie des familles nobles de France (page 195).
[80] Les d'Estrées: leurs domains et leurs liens de parenté au pays de Bray (Haute-Normandie): Notes généalogiques et historiques oar un Neufchatellois (page 10).
[81] http://fr.wikipedia.org/wiki/Jean_Ier_d'Estr%C3%A9es
[82] http://racineshistoire.free.fr/LGN/PDF/Estrees.pdf (pg 3)

After serving as high page to Queen Anne of Bretagne, the wife of King Louis XII, he also served under King François I and King Henri III. [83] [84]

Appointed Grand Master of the Artillery of France, under the reign of Henri II, on July 9, 1550, [85] [86] as Captain of Folembray in 1556, he also assisted in the capture of Calais in 1558. [87] [88]

---

[83] Les d'Estrées: leurs domains et leurs liens de parenté au pays de Bray (Haute-Normandie): Notes généalogiques et historiques oar un Neufchatellois (page 11).
[84] François-Alexandre Aubert de la Chesnaye des Bois (1773). Dictionnaire de la noblesse, contenant les généalogies, l'histoire et la chronologie des familles nobles de France (page 195).
[85] Les d'Estrées: leurs domains et leurs liens de parenté au pays de Bray (Haute-Normandie): Notes généalogiques et historiques oar un Neufchatellois (page 11).
[86] François-Alexandre Aubert de la Chesnaye des Bois (1773). Dictionnaire de la noblesse, contenant les généalogies, l'histoire et la chronologie des familles nobles de France (page 195).
[87] Les d'Estrées: leurs domains et leurs liens de parenté au pays de Bray (Haute-Normandie): Notes généalogiques et historiques oar un Neufchatellois (page 11).

He held the formal titles of Count of Orbec, Marquis of Coeuvres, Seigneur de Valieu, Baron de Doudeauville en Boulonnais and Viscount of Soissons. [89]

Having saved the life of Jacques de Bourbon, bastard of Vendôme, Seigneur de Bonneval, Seigneur de Ligny and Seigneur de Lambercourt (husband of Jeanne Rubempré), he married Catherine de Bourbon-Vendôme, the eldest daughter, about 1515; they had three children, one son and two daughters. [90]

Jean I d'Estrées had embraced Calvinism.

[5] Antoine IV d'Estrées, Marquis of Coeuvres, Viscount of Soissons, married Françoise Babou, daughter of Jean Babou (Baron de Sagonne, Seigneur de la Bourdaisière, Seigneur

---

[88] François-Alexandre Aubert de la Chesnaye des Bois (1773). <u>Dictionnaire de la noblesse, contenant les généalogies, l'histoire et la chronologie des familles nobles de France</u> (page 195).
[89] Les d'Estrées: leurs domains et leurs liens de parenté au pays de Bray (Haute-Normandie): Notes généalogiques et historiques oar un Neufchatellois (pages 10 and 11).
[90] http://racineshistoire.free.fr/LGN/PDF/Estrees.pdf (pg 3)

de Thuisseau and Ambassador to Rome) on February 14, 1559. [91] [92] [93]

In addition to his familial titles, denoted previously, when he married my mother, he was Governor and Seneschal of the Boulonnais as well as Governor of La Fère, Paris and Île de France; he later became Grand Master of the Artillery of France (from 1597 to 1599) under the reign of Henri VI. [94] [95]

Of the nine children born of this union, seven were female. [96] [97]

1° François-Louis

2° François-Annibal I

---

[91] http://racineshistoire.free.fr/LGN/PDF/Estrees.pdf (pg 3)
[92] http://www.thepeerage.com/p59.htm#i587
[93] Les d'Estrées: leurs domains et leurs liens de parenté au pays de Bray (Haute-Normandie): Notes généalogiques et historiques oar un Neufchatellois (page 14).
[94] Ibid.
[95] http://en.wikipedia.org/wiki/Antoine_d'Estr%C3%A9es
[96] http://racineshistoire.free.fr/LGN/PDF/Estrees.pdf (pg 4)
[97] François-Alexandre Aubert de la Chesnaye des Bois (1773). Dictionnaire de la noblesse, contenant les généalo-gies, l'histoire et la chronologie des familles nobles de France (page 196).

3° Diane

4° Marguerite

5° Angélique

6° Gabrielle (me)

7° Julienne-Hippolyte

8° Marie-Françoise

9° Marie-Catherine

As you will see, so, too, is my paternal grandmother's lineage an ancient and prestigious one.

King Louis IX married Marguerite de Provence
Robert de France, Seigneur de Bourbon, married Beatrix de Bourgogne [98]
Louis I de Bourbon, Duc de Bourbon, married Marie de Hainaut [99]
Jacques I de Bourbon, Comte de La Marche, married Jeanne de Châtillon [100]

---

[98] http://racineshistoire.free.fr/LGN/PDF/Bourbon-duche.pdf (page 2)
[99] http://racineshistoire.free.fr/LGN/PDF/Bourbon-duche.pdf (page 2)

Jean de Bourbon La Marche, Comte de La Marche, married Catherine, Comtesse de Vendôme [101]
Louis I de Bourbon-Vendôme, Comte de Vendôme, married Blanche de Roucy [102]
Jean II de Bourbon-Vendôme, Comte de Vendôme, had a liason with Philippine de Gournay [103]
Jacques de Bourbon-Vendôme, Seigneur de Bonneval, married Jeanne, Dame de Rubempré [104]
Catherine de Bourbon-Vendôme married Jean d'Estrées, Seigneur de Coeuvres, my paternal grandfather [105]

Jacques de Bourbon, bastard of Vendôme, my paternal great grandfather, had been legitimized by Letters of Patent from the King on December 1518. [106] As a result of Jean d'Estrées, now married to his eldest daughter, so, too, did this mean that he had become the cousin of Charles de Bourbon-Vendôme, grandfather of King Henri IV of France,

---

[100] http://racineshistoire.free.fr/LGN/PDF/Bourbon-duche.pdf (page 3)

[101] Ibid, page 11.

[102] Ibid, page 12.

[103] Ibid, page 14.

[104] Ibid.

[105] Ibid, page 21.

[106] Les d'Estrées: leurs domains et leurs liens de parenté au pays de Bray (Haute-Normandie): Notes généalogiques et historiques oar un Neufchatellois (page 13).

through marriage, as the following will attest. In keeping, Henri IV and I were cousins.

Louis I de Bourbon-Vendôme, Comte de Vendôme, married firstly Blanche de Roucy [107]	Louis I de Bourbon-Vendôme, Comte de Vendôme, married secondly Jeanne de Laval [108]
Jean II de Bourbon-Vendôme, Comte de Vendôme, had a liason with Philippine de Gournay [109]	Jean VII de Bourbon-Vendôme, Comte de Vendôme, married Isabel de Beauvau [110]
Jacques de Bourbon-Vendôme, Seigneur de Bonneval, married Jeanne, Dame de Rubempré [111]	François I de Bourbon, Comte de La Marche et Vendôme, married Marie de Luxembourg [112] [113]
Catherine de Bourbon-Vendôme married Jean d'Estrées, Seigneur de Coeuvres (my paternal grandfather) [114]	Charles I de Bourbon, Duc de Vendôme, Duc de Bourbon, married Françoise d'Alençon [115] [116]

---

[107] http://racineshistoire.free.fr/LGN/PDF/Bourbon-duche.pdf (page 12)
[108] Ibid.
[109] Ibid, page 14.
[110] Ibid.
[111] Ibid.
[112] Ibid.
[113] http://racineshistoire.free.fr/LGN/PDF/Bourbon-Dynastie-Royale.pdf (page 2)
[114] http://racineshistoire.free.fr/LGN/PDF/Bourbon-duche.pdf (page 21)

Antoine IV d'Estrées, my father	Antoine de Bourbon married Jeanne III d'Albret, Queen of Navarre [117] [118]
Gabrielle d'Estrées, myself	Henri IV, King of France and Navarre [119]

At sixteen, I was chatelaine of our home, the Château de Coeuvres-et-Valsery; called *La Belle Gabrielle*, I rather came to detest the name.

Father had seen to it that I had been trained to defend our home against mauraders. I knew how to apply the match to the culverin, [120] how to fire an arquebuse, [121] and how to defend myself with a dagger.

---

[115] http://racineshistoire.free.fr/LGN/PDF/Bourbon-duche.pdf (page 18)

[116] http://racineshistoire.free.fr/LGN/PDF/Bourbon-Dynastie-Royale.pdf (page 2)

[117] Ibid, page 19.

[118] http://racineshistoire.free.fr/LGN/PDF/Bourbon-Dynastie-Royale.pdf (page 2)

[119] Ibid, page 3.

[120] http://en.wikipedia.org/wiki/Culverin

[121] http://en.wikipedia.org/wiki/Arquebus

Companion to my father, I always accompanied him on the hunting and hawking parties; our favorite recreation activity. Often a boisterous occasion, so, too, was it tempered with the courtliness of manners; we were, after all, the feudal lords and ladies of our day.

I was a mere eighteen years when Henri and I first met in 1591. By comparison, Henri was a seasoned thirty-eight.

As King of Navarre, he was a king without a kingdom for Pope Sixtus V had excommunicated him in 1585, giving the kingdom of Navarre to Spain and declaring him unworthy of the French crown.

When first we met, Henri had a worn and aged look about him, due to the excessive fatigue brought on by the disquietudes of civil war; a war that was centered upon a perpetual clash of opinions.

However, *never* did I witness the exudance of a defeatist attitude.

His was a visage that was furrowed with wrinkles, hardened by constant exposure to the elements and darkened to the point of blackness. In fact, if not for the buoyancy, and conviction, of his spirits, I would have taken him for a much older man.

In addition, the extreme bodily exertion and mental anxiety that was the basis for his everyday existence gave way to the graying of hair, beard and mustache.

With piercing black eyes, so, too, were they keen and playful, understanding and gentle. His countenance was one of banter and good humor.

In truth, he exuded an air of utter dauntlessness.

Whilest I had first thought him the ugliest gentleman in all of France, so, too, did he present himself as the bravest of knights in the realm.

The wonderful orator of many great stories, stories of love and war, we listened with great abandon, for they were told with unstudied eloquence; his was the laughter that elevated our spirits.

It was during the course of one of his mirthful recitals, his weather-worn lit up with such animation, coupled with the intense merriment of his eyes, that I came to see the handsomeness of the man; so, too, was this when I fell in love with Henri.

After having disclosed my true feelings, I learned that Henri had fallen in love with me, when first we met.

Married in 1592, to Nicolas de Lamerval, Seigneur de Liancourt, I had reached the age of nineteen years; this was none other than a marriage of convenience.

It was Henri himself who had arranged the marriage to this rich and influential family, so that my father need no longer worry about the fact that Henri, being but a poor and excommunicated heretic, had little hope of ever becoming accepted as king of France; in truth, it had been arranged so that we could escape the severe scrutiny of my father.

At the tender age of twenty, in 1593, Henri and I became lovers.

Henri was able to see past my persona of noble beauty, grace and sweetness of temper, inherited from my mother, to the fiercely loyal, intelligent and practical woman that I was; all courtesy of my father's influence.

I liked not my blue eyes and hair of fine spun gold, mainly because I detested being stared at.

Henri had disclosed, to me, that Henri III of France, upon his deathbed, shared words of wisdom with him … *Mon bon frère Henriot, tu ne seras jamais roi de France, si tu ne deviens pas Catholique.*

In my desire to see Henri as more than *titular* king of France, I counselled him to embrace Catholicism.

He knew that he had but two choices; he could either renounce the crown or he could adopt the predominant faith of the people.

Recognizing the wisdom of my argument, it was on July 25, 1593 that Henri declared *Paris to be well worth a Mass.*

Perhaps it was in the relief of Henri having permanently renounced Protestantism, finally ending the religious wars, that I found myself pregnant, with our first child, several months later.

On February 27, 1594, Henri was formally crowned as King of France. It was this same year that Henri also arranged for the annullment of my marriage to Liancourt.

Our children were ......

[1] César de Bourbon, born June 3, 1594; it was on January 4, 1595, that Henri officially recognized and legitimized our son in a text validated by the *Parlement de Paris*; he was created the first Duc de Vendôme, by his father in 1598.

[2] Catherine Henriette de Bourbon, born November 11, 1596; our daughter was declared legitimate on November 17, 1596 at the Abbey of St. Ouen in Rouen.

[3] Alexandre de Bourbon, also legitimized and titled Chevalier de Vendôme, born in 1598.

Our relationship, however, did not sit well with some members of the French aristocracy wherein I had earned the nickname *la duchesse d'Ordure*, meaing the Duchess of Filth; this simply made them stare even more.

As Henri's most important diplomat, I began to make use of many female friends, amongst the various Catholic League families, to bring about peace.

In 1598, Henri issued the *Edict of Nantes*, according the Calvinist Protestants of France (also known as French Huguenots) substantial rights in a nation that was considered essentially Catholic.

Having joined forces with Catherine de Bourbon, sister to Henri, together we went to work overriding the objections of some of the more powerful Catholic and Huguenot families, forcing both factions to comply with the edict.

It was after applying to Pope Clement VIII for an annulment of his marriage to Marguerite that, in March 1599, Henri presented me with his coronation ring.

At long last, we were making plans to reign together as King and Queen of France.

In November 1598, newly pregnant with our fourth child, I moved into the official bedchamber reserved for the Queen.

Alas, I was not meant to be Queen, for I suffered an attack of eclampsia, on April 9, giving birth to a stillborn son.

http://img.xooimage.com/files21/7/7/d/gabrielle_d_estrees-
11a562e.jpg

http://www.pourlhistoire.com/images/margot/henri%204.jpg

Concluding Message

Returning from memories such as these is always difficult.

I now understand why Ghislain was so haunted; he had been forbidden to disclose any information as to the lives we had shared.

The ring that served as the trigger mechanism was, in actual fact, the coronation ring that Henri had given me over four hundred years previous.

I now know that I have always been the Queen of his heart.

I trust that you have enjoyed this story of my rememberance.

Ysabeau Gabrielle LeBlanc

Mu, The Motherland

Many are of the opinion (and belief) that Lemuria is the name of a hypothetical lost land, situated somewhere in the Indian and Pacific oceans, its precise locale, in ancient times, unknown.

The JOIDES Resolution (Joint Oceanographic Institutions for Deep Earth Sampling) is a scientific drilling ship that has been utilized to conduct research.

In 1999, drilling discovered evidence that a large island, [122] the Kerguelen Plateau, was submerged about 20 million years ago, unbeknownst to the larger scientific community.

In truth, can it not be said that there still exist many things of which we know naught?

In accordance with a Tamil tradition, Kumari Kandam, a legendary sunken kingdom, is sometimes compared to Lemuria. [123] [124] Referred to as the Land of Purity, this was a sophisticated kingdom of higher learning.

While this was *not* Lemuria, there were many similarities between these two lands.

During a most violent catastrophe of a geological nature, the entire island was submerged under water.

---

[122] Lost Continent Discovered. BBC News. 27 May 1999. Retrieved on November 30, 2010 from http://news.bbc.co.uk/2/hi/science/nature/353277.stm

[123] http://www.youtube.com/watch?v=PZKiCpFisoY

[124] http://www.thehindu.com/news/national/tamil-nadu/lemuria-and-kumari-kandam/article482101.ece

It has been said that the remaining survivors migrated to the Indian continent (of today), sparking the historically documented Indus Valley Civilization of 3300 to 1300 BCE.

Contrary to popular belief, the original continent of Mu was not located in the Pacific; it was a grand unified land mass that included South America, Africa, India and Australia. When separation occurred, this original continent split, forming most of the continents that we see today. [125]

A Short History of Lemuria [126]

Different Theories About Lemuria [127]

---

[125] http://starchildglobal.com/starchild/lemurians.html
[126] http://esoterism.ro/english/lemuria.php
[127]

http://www.bibliotecapleyades.net/atlantida_mu/esp_lemuria_2.htm

Geological Evidence Lemuria Actually Existed [128]

Kryon Questions and Answers [129]

Legend of Lemuria [130]

Lemuria [131] [132] [133] [134]

Lemurian Scrolls (Satguru Sivaya Subramuniyaswami) [135]

Lemuria, the Continent of Mu [136]

---

[128] http://mitchtestone.blogspot.ca/2011/08/lemuria-actually-existed-geologic.html

[129] http://kryon.com/inspiritmag/archives/Q-A%20archives/Q-A-archive.html

[130] http://www.absoluteempowerment.com/Lemuria.php

[131] http://www.crystalinks.com/lemuria.html

[132] http://en.wikipedia.org/wiki/Lemuria_(continent)

[133] http://www.juneaustin.co.uk/ancient-civilisations/lemuria

[134] http://lemuria-kumarinadu.blogspot.ca/

[135] http://www.kundaliniawakeningsystems1.com/downloads/lemurian-scrolls_-_angelic_prophecies_revealing_human_origins_rev1.1.pdf

[136] http://www.bibliotecapleyades.net/esp_lemuria.htm

Ad Infinitum: Unchanging and Forevermore

---

[137] http://www.burlingtonnews.net/leumurian1.html
[138] http://www.generationspirit.com/spiritual-men/61-messages-from-kryon-an-interview-with-lee-carroll
[139] http://kryon.com/k_25.html
[140] http://newdimension2012.blogspot.ca/2012/12/some-thoughts-about-lemuria-and-atlantis.html
[141] http://www.kryon.com/k_channel12_Patagonia-bigpicture.html
[142]

http://www.bibliotecapleyades.net/esp_lemuria.htm#menu
[143] http://www.youtube.com/watch?v=V0WNPSnMGZ4
[144]

http://www.bibliotecapleyades.net/sociopolitica/the_experiment/experiment.htm#contents

The History of Humanity [145]

The Lemuria / Atlantis Conflict [146]

The Lemurian Connection [147]

The Lost Continent of Lemuria [148]

The Lost Lands of Mu and Lemuria [149]

The Lost Lemuria [150] [151]

The Pineal Tones™ [152] [153]

---

[145] http://www.kryon.com/k_chanelcruise8.html

[146] http://www.neweraenergyinstitute.com/Lemuria_Atlantis_Extract.pdf

[147] http://www.lemurianconnection.com/category/about-lemuria-and-telos/

[148] http://themindunleashed.org/2013/08/the-lost-continent-of-lemuria.html

[149] http://www.redicecreations.com/article.php?id=1759

[150] http://www.sacred-texts.com/atl/tll/tll02.htm

[151] http://www.jasoncolavito.com/the-lost-lemuria.html

[152] http://www.lemurianchoir.com/the-pineal-tones

[153] http://www.pineal-tones.com/pinealtones/listen-here/

Ad Infinitum: Unchanging and Forevermore

The Solar Brotherhood of the Seven Rays [154]

The Sounds of Lemuria (Jonathan Goldman) [155]

The Timing of Creation: The Lemurian Awakening [156]

---

[154] http://www.wolflodge.org/sananda/Brotherhood-Rays.htm
[155] http://www.healingsounds.com/what-were-the-sounds-of-lemuria
[156] https://www.kryon.com/k_channel12_Hawaii-1.html

Lemurian Seed Crystals

Lemurian Seed Crystals are a special variety of clear Quartz crystals that have been found in the Diamantina region of Brazil. These crystals display some very unique ladder like groove markings.

Many individuals, myself included, are drawn to the fabled land of Lemuria; an ancient civilization also known as Mu (meaning the Motherland), believed to have sunk beneath the Pacific Ocean thousands of years ago. In fact, it is said that the volcanoes of Hawaii, as well as other Polynesian islands, are, in fact, the tops of ancient Lemurian mountains.

Lemuria has been touted as a civilization whereby one felt in touch with the Divine as well as the totality of all life; the very same spiritual consciousness that many are striving for today.

Could it be that Lemuria was the basis for the Garden of Eden, making this a very real place?

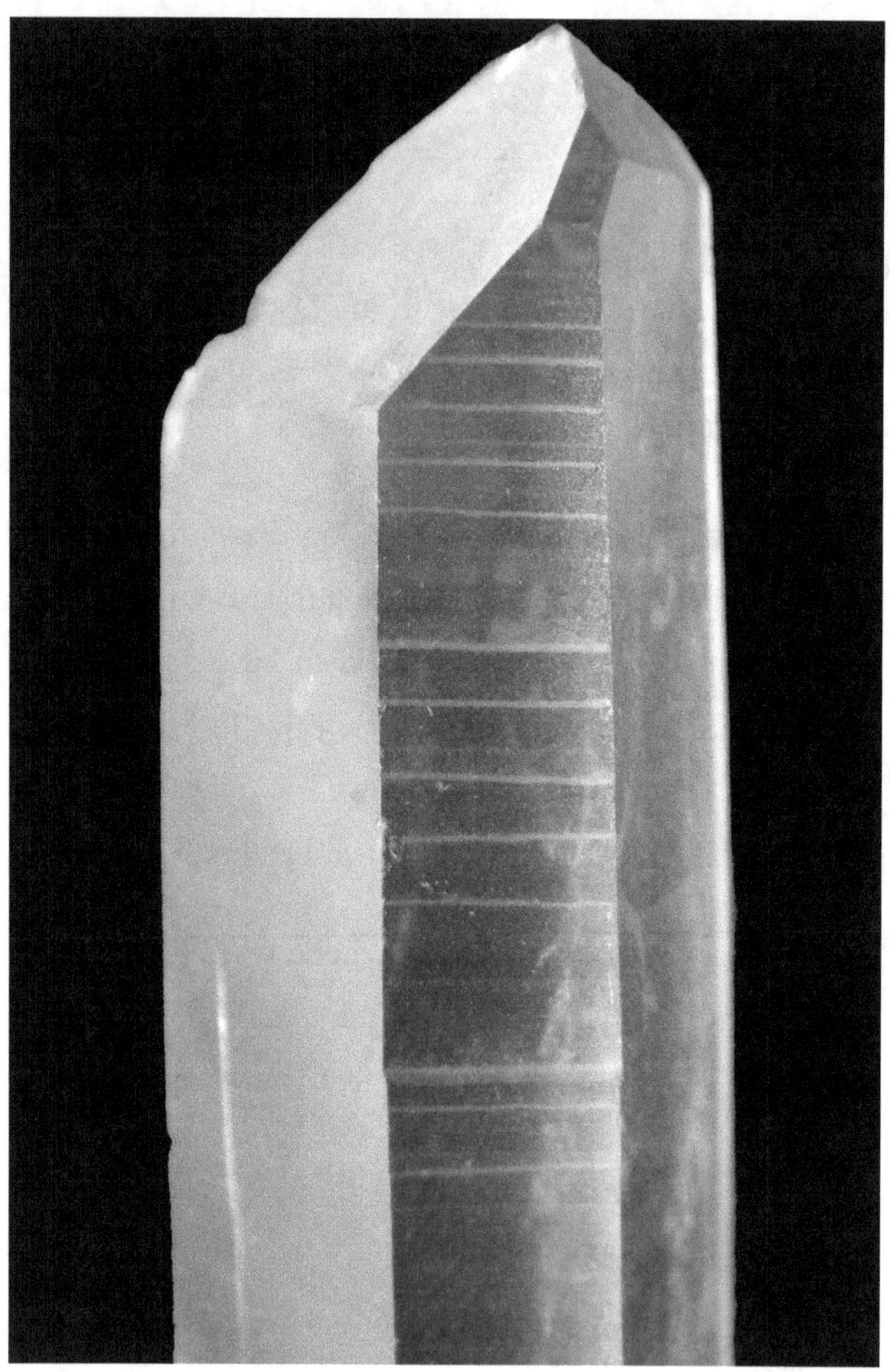

It has been said that these particular crystals are encoded with the vibrations of Lemurian consciousness; a consciousness that was based upon heart connection with Spirit. It can easily be concluded, therefore, that the Lemurians were emotionally centered individuals with a strong spiritual consciousness.

During the last days of Lemuria, it was decided to plant seed crystals programmed to transmit a message of oneness. Having seeded the crystals, the Lemurians, it is believed, left this planet for other star systems. Others went into inner earth (while maintaining telepathic connection with those in other parts of the galaxy), where they continue to care for the earth and the seed crystals now surfacing.

When working with these crystals in meditation, I feel more whole as a person.

I also feel balanced (physical, mental, emotional, spiritual) on all levels.

While the energies may be soft and loving, feminine in nature, they are also intensely powerful.

I enjoy working with these specialty crystals when conducting long distance Reiki energy sends.

A caretaker to numerous Lemurian Seed Crystals, I chose to meditate with the very first being that came to live with me.

We are addressing you, Starwalker, for you, too, have come from the stars.

You are the very essence of the universe, comprised of the same stardust as all of creation.

Reaching for, achieving and attaining, the quiet within is what replenishes the well.

The challenge, especially in these times, lies in finding the time and space in which to reach this knowing state, and yet it is imperative that you do so.

You must take the time out of your hectic, fast paced, stressful lives (of your own creation) in order to do so. Life is simply what you make it.

Ad Infinitum: Unchanging and Forevermore

In your stargazing on a clear night, have you ever wondered from whence you came from before braving it all to travel to the faculty of earth? Everyone knows that earth is the school that most elect to enroll in, knowing, full well, that one's experience here is not always an easy one. That is why you committed yourself to coming and we hereby salute you.

If it is your wish to recreate the Garden of Eden prototype within your current existence, you must begin by reclaiming your power, by thinking and responding for yourselves.

You must be willing to step away from the herd in order to start thinking outside the box (pen), for this has served to enslave you to a power that exists outside of yourselves.

Might it be that this original enslavement was what you have termed the fall from grace?

Stand tall.

Stand firm in what you believe, knowing that you are on the road to remembrance.

Graduating from an ego based consciousness to a heart centered consciousness shall become your earned degree.

It is up to you to reconnect with, and start remembering, that which has long been forgotten.

There was a time when peace enveloped the entirety of this planet; a time of considerable spiritual consciousness.

Some of you may actually remember the time of this past golden age. So, too, is there to be another time when peace shall reign supreme once more, and that time is now.

Do not allow another to create your reality for you. It is up to you to create that which you envision for yourself.

Believe. Act according to the dictates of your heart. Give thanks for the denoted outcome.

We are but here to assist, as crystalline midwives, in its birthing. As you will it, so shall it be.

The Armana Dynasty

Amenhotep III, also known as Amenhotep the Magnificent, was the father of Akhenaten.

Amenhotep III enjoyed the distinction of having the most surviving statues (over 250) of any Egyptian pharaoh having been discovered and identified; since these statues span his entire life, they provide a series of portraits covering the entirety of his reign. [157]

His lengthy reign was a period of unprecedented prosperity and artistic splendour, when Egypt reached the peak of her artistic and international power. [158]

Proof of this is shown by the diplomatic correspondence from the rulers of Assyria, Mitanni, Babylon, and Hatti, which is preserved in the archive of the Amarna Letters.

---

[157] http://en.wikipedia.org/wiki/Amenhotep_iii
[158] Ibid.

These letters (covering the period from Year 30 of Amenhotep III until at least the end of Akhenaten's reign) document frequent requests by these rulers for gold and numerous other gifts from the pharaoh. [159]

When Amenhotep III died, [160] he left behind a country that was at the very height of its power and influence, commanding immense respect in the international world; however, he also bequeathed an Egypt that was wedded to its traditional political and religious certainties under the Amun priesthood. [161]

The resulting upheavals from his son Akhenaten's reforming zeal would shake these old certainties to their very foundations and bring forth the central question of whether a pharaoh was more powerful than the existing

---

[159] http://en.wikipedia.org/wiki/Amenhotep_iii
[160] http://www.osirisnet.net/tombes/pharaons/amenhotep3/e_am enhotep3.htm
[161] http://en.wikipedia.org/wiki/Amenhotep_iii

domestic order as represented by the Amun priests and their numerous temple estates. [162]

Akhenaten even moved the capital away from the city of Thebes in an effort to break the influence of that powerful temple and assert his own preferred choice of deities, [163] at the site known today as Amarna.

Tiye, the Great Royal Wife of Amenhotep III, was the daughter of Yuya and Thuya.

It sometimes is suggested that Tiye's father, Yuya, was of Asiatic or Nubian descent due to the features of his mummy and the many different spellings of his name, which might imply it was a non-Egyptian name in origin. [164]

---

[162] http://en.wikipedia.org/wiki/Amenhotep_iii
[163] http://www.osirisnet.net/docu/akhenat/e_akhen1.htm
[164] http://en.wikipedia.org/wiki/Tiye

In 2003, Dr. Joann Fletcher took part in a controversial expedition to the Valley of the Kings in Egypt, where she claimed to have found the mummy of Queen Nefertiti, identified as the Younger Woman, among the cache in tomb KV35. [165]

Dr. Zahi Hawass identified the Younger Woman as a middle-aged woman, Merytre-Hatshepsut (also referred to as Hatshepsut-Merytre), the main wife of king Tuthmosis III; however, the DNA tests published in early 2010 (in an article co-authored by Hawass) have proven that the Younger Woman mummy was *both a sister of Akhenaten as well as the mother of Tutankhamun,* [166] more than likely a minor wife, given that Akhenaten and Queen Nefertiti were not related. [167]

---

[165] http://en.wikipedia.org/wiki/Joann_Fletcher
[166] Ibid.
[167]

http://jama.jamanetwork.com/article.aspx?articleid=185393

KV35 [168]

Featured left to right

Elder Lady, young unidentified boy, Younger Lady

Boasting long reddish hair falling across her shoulders, the Elder Lady (KV35EL) mummy was identified, in February 2010, by DNA testing, as Queen Tiye, the daughter of Yuya

---

[168]

http://anubis4_2000.tripod.com/mummypages2/KV35Mum miesColor.jpg and Thuya, wife of Amenhotep III, and mother of Akhenaten. [169] [170]

This image of Queen Tiye can be found at the Egyptian Museum in Berlin.

The tomb of Yuya and Thuya was, until the discovery of Tutankhamun's, one of the most spectacular ever found in the Valley of the Kings despite the fact that Yuya was never pharaoh. [171]

169
http://jama.jamanetwork.com/article.aspx?articleid=185393
[170] http://news.discovery.com/history/king-tut-grandmother-mummy-wart-110322.html
[171] http://en.wikipedia.org/wiki/Yuya

Although the burial site was robbed in antiquity, many objects not considered valuable by the robbers still remained; both mummies, largely intact, were in an amazing state of preservation. [172]

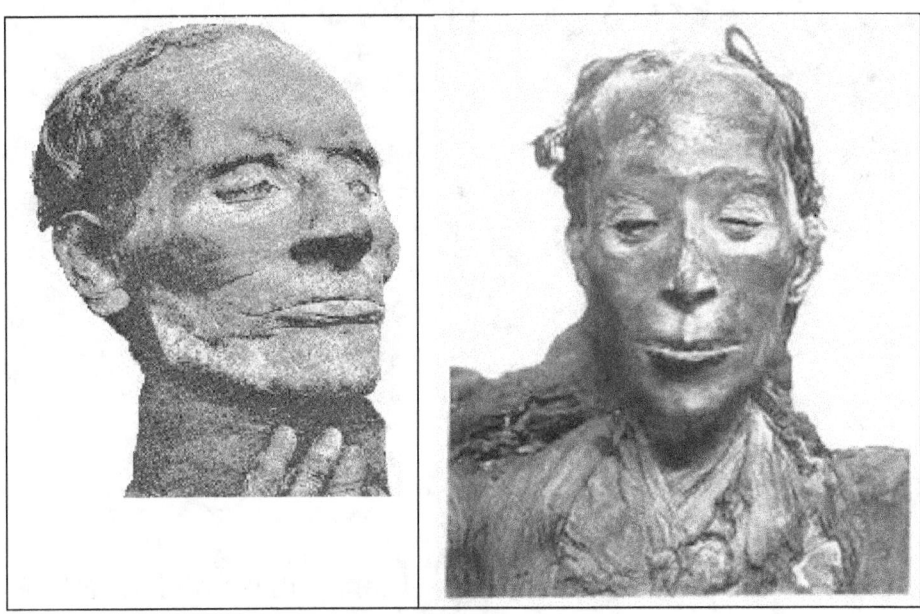

Mummy of Yuya [173]

Mummy of Thuya [174]

---

[172] http://en.wikipedia.org/wiki/Yuya
[173] http://michellemoran.com/books/nefertiti/behind-the-story/family-mummies.html
[174] Ibid.

Mummy mask of Yuya [175]   Mummy mask of Thuya [176]

175

http://en.wikipedia.org/wiki/File:Mummy_mask_of_Yuya.jp
g
176

http://en.wikipedia.org/wiki/File:Mummy_mask_of_Thuya.j
pg

As Yuya and Thuya were the parents of Queen Tiye; so, too, were they the likely parents of Vizier Ay.

While Yuya lived in Upper Egypt, an area that was predominantly native Egyptian, he could have been an assimilated descendant of Asiatic immigrants or slaves who rose to become a member of the local nobility at Akhmin. [177]

If he was not a foreigner, however, then Yuya would have been the native Egyptian whose daughter was married to Amenhotep III. [178]

It was not typical for an Egyptian person to have so many different ways to write his name, suggesting that Yuya's ancestors had a foreign origin. [179]

---

[177] http://en.wikipedia.org/wiki/Yuya
[178] Ibid.
[179] Ibid.

Journalist, and author, Ahmed Osman has even suggested an identification between Joseph, the ancient Hebrew patriarch who led the tribe of Israel into Egypt during a famine, and Yuya. [180]

Through analysis of anomalous features of the mummy of Yuya, as well as linguistic and chronological data, Osman points out how Yuya is the only Egyptian mummy to have his hands placed under his chin rather than across his chest; he also has what appears to be Semetic features, along with a beard style similar to that of the ancient Hebrews, whereas Egyptian officials were known to shave their facial hair. [181]

His wife, Thuya is believed to be a descendant of Queen Ahmose-Nefertari, wife of Ahmose I. [182]

---

[180] http://en.wikipedia.org/wiki/Yuya
[181] Ibid.
[182] http://en.wikipedia.org/wiki/Tjuyu

Amenhotep IV, also known as Akhenaten, tried to bring about a departure from traditional religion, [183] yet in the end it would not be accepted. [184]

After his death, [185] traditional religious practice was gradually restored, and when, some dozen years later, rulers without clear rights of succession from the Eighteenth Dynasty founded a new dynasty, they discredited Akhenaten and his immediate successors, referring to Akhenaten himself as *the enemy* in archival records. [186]

The term talatat (a word that may have been derived from *tagliata* meaning *cut masonry*) was used by ancient Egyptian workmen. [187]

---

[183] http://www.osirisnet.net/docu/akhenat/e_akhen1.htm
[184] http://en.wikipedia.org/wiki/Amenhotep_IV
[185]

http://www.osirisnet.net/tombes/amarna/akhenaton/e_akhentomb.htm
[186] http://en.wikipedia.org/wiki/Amenhotep_IV
[187] http://en.wikipedia.org/wiki/Talatat

These stone blocks, of standardized size, were used during the reign of Akhenaten in the building of the Aten temples at both Armana and Karnack. [188]

As purported by Josh Bernstein, Akhenaten was the *first* Pharaoh to make use of this type of block, primarily because he was trying to create art and architecture, at Armana, in such a short period of time. [189]

With each block weighing approximately 100 pounds, the carrying of the finished blocks, probably for several miles, became the real challenge; Akhenaten wanted the city of Armana built quickly and to his specifications, thereby placing incredible physical, and severely punishing, demands on his people. [190]

---

[188] http://en.wikipedia.org/wiki/Talatat
[189] *Into the Unknown with Josh Berstein: Egypt's Lost King* (a documentary that explored the controversial Pharaoh, Akhenaten) Season 1, Episode 5 (aired September 16, 2008).
[190] Ibid.

The Director of the Armana Project, Professor Barry Kemp (also an archaeologist) from the University of Cambridge in the UK, has shared that during the time of Akhenaten, Armana was a barren desert, a harsh environment, a most inhospitable place for over 30,000 followers. [191]

In accordance with the Armana Project findings, these people were among the shortest people in ancient Egyptian history, both before and after Akhenaten's time, by at least 6 inches, which could well have been attributed to a prolonged malnutritional problem. [192]

Coupled with a premature death age of about thirty-two, there was also a high rate of spinal trauma, most probably associated with heavy lifting. [193]

---

[191] *Into the Unknown with Josh Berstein: Egypt's Lost King* (a documentary that explored the controversial Pharaoh, Akhenaten) Season 1, Episode 5 (aired September 16, 2008).
[192] Ibid.
[193] Ibid.

It was Sigmund Freud, the founder of psychoanalysis, who, in his book <u>Moses and Monotheism</u>, argued that Moses had been an Atenist priest forced to leave Egypt with his followers after Akhenaten's death. [194]

Freud also argued that Akhenaten was striving to promote monotheism, something that the biblical Moses was able to achieve; following this book, the concept entered popular consciousness and serious research. [195]

Abundant visual imagery of the Aten disk was central to Atenism, which celebrated the natural world. [196]

Interestingly, pottery found throughout Judea, dating to the end of the 8th century BC, has seals resembling a winged sun disk burned on their handles; so, too, are these said to be the royal seal of the Judean Kingdom. [197]

---

[194] http://en.wikipedia.org/wiki/Amenhotep_IV
[195] Ibid.
[196] Ibid.
[197] Ibid.

Might there be a connection, after all, as argued by journalist, and author, Ahmed Osman?

Based on the rather strange and eccentric portrayals of Akhenaten, with a sagging stomach, thick thighs, larger breasts, and long, thin face (so different from the athletic norm in the portrayal of Pharaohs), it was suggested that Akhenaten may have suffered from Marfan's Syndrome; however, this was ruled out following DNA tests on Tutankhamun in 2010. [198]

Dominic Montserrat in <u>Akhenaten: History, Fantasy and Ancient Egypt</u> argued that "there is now a broad consensus among Egyptologists that the exaggerated forms of Akhenaten's physical portrayal ... are not to be read literally." [199]

---

[198] http://en.wikipedia.org/wiki/Amenhotep_IV
[199] Ibid.

In keeping, Montserrats believes that the body shape relates to some form of religious symbolism. [200]

Knowing that the god Aten was referred to as *the mother and father of all humankind* it has been suggested that Akhenaten was made to look androgynous, in artwork, as a symbol of the androgyny of the god. [201]

Akhenaten's chief wife, on countless monuments, is shown to be Nefertiti, [202] a name that means *the beauty has come.* [203]

Nowhere is the parentage of Nefertiti stated; in addition, the fact that she is never called King's Daughter or King's Sister makes it certain that she was not of royal birth. [204]

---

[200] http://en.wikipedia.org/wiki/Amenhotep_IV

[201] Ibid.

[202] Dodson, Aidan and Hilton, Dyan. (2004) <u>The Complete Royal Families of Ancient Egypt</u> (page 146). London, UK: Thames & Hudson Ltd.

[203] http://en.wikipedia.org/wiki/Nefertiti

A clue, however, may lie in the fact that a lady named Tey is referred to as Nefertiti's nurse on a number of the queen's monuments. [205]

We know Tey's husband to have been Ay, whose title of God's Father is sometimes one that refers to being the father of a queen.

It has been suggested that Nefertiti may have been a daughter of Ay (who, in turn, was the son of Yuya and Thuya), perhaps by a wife who died in childbirth; meaning that Tey was another wife who actually brought up the queen. [206] [207]

---

[204] Dodson, Aidan and Hilton, Dyan. (2004) The Complete Royal Families of Ancient Egypt (page 146). London, UK: Thames & Hudson Ltd.

[205] Ibid.

[206] Ibid, page 147.

[207] http://en.wikipedia.org/wiki/Ay

Nefertiti [208]

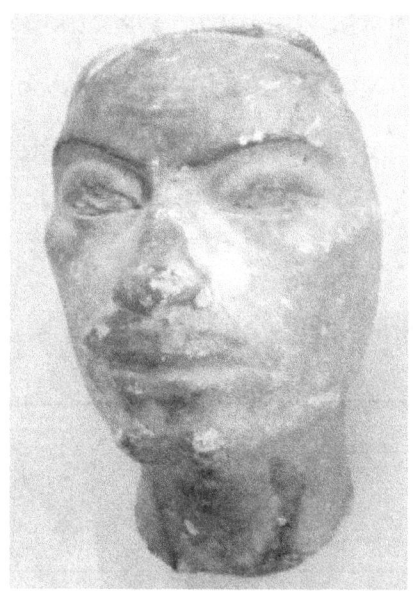

Portrait of a man thought to be Ay [209]

208

http://farm1.static.flickr.com/12/18780827_581c8feecf.jpg

Akhenaton [210]

---

[209] http://en.wikipedia.org/wiki/File:PortraitStudyOfAy.png

[210]

http://www4.images.coolspotters.com/wallpapers/75375/akh enaten-mobile-wallpaper.jpg

Akhenaton [211]

[211]

http://www.usu.edu/markdamen/1320Hist&Civ/slides/10akh
en/akhenaten1osirid.jpg

Nefertiti bust [212]

Altes Museum in Berlin

Part of the Ägyptisches Museum Berlin collection

212

http://www.smb.museum/smb/sammlungen/details.php?objI
D=2&n=0&r=0&p=24

Nefertiti bust [213]

Altes Museum in Berlin

Part of the Ägyptisches Museum Berlin collection

---

[213] http://www.egyptian-museum-berlin.com/c53.php

In keeping with JAMA, the <u>Journal of the American Medical Association</u>, an article entitled "Ancestry and Pathology in King Tutankhamun's Family" was published in the February 17, 2010 issue (Volume 303, No. 7). [214]

Between September 2007 and October 2009, Zahi Hawass, Yehia Z. Gad, Somaia Ismail and other members of the team (from Egypt, Germany, and Italy) independently examined 11 royal mummies, believed to be from King Tutankhamun's immediate lineage (circa 1410 to 1324 BC) as well as another 5 royal mummies from an earlier period (circa 1550 to 1479 BC). [215] [216]

<u>Putative Members of the Tutankhamun Lineage</u>

[1] Tutankhamun (KV62)

214

http://jama.jamanetwork.com/article.aspx?articleid=185393
[215] Ibid.
216

http://jama.jamanetwork.com/article.aspx?articleid=185374

[2] Yuya (KV46)

[3] Amenhotep III (KV35)

[4] Akhenaten (KV55)

[5] Thuya (KV46)

[6] Tiye (KV35EL)

[7] unknown female (KV35YL)

[8] unknown female (KV21A)

[9] unknown female (KV21B)

[10] stillbirth Fetus 1 (KV62)

[11] stillbirth Fetus 2 (KV62)

Morphological and Genetic Control Group (5 royal mummies from an earlier period)

[1] Ahmose-Nefertari (TT320) (CCG61055)

[2] Thutmose II (TT320) (CCG61066)

[3] unknown male (TT320) (CCG61065)

[4] Hatshepsut (KV60A)

[5] Sitra-In (KV60B) royal wet-nurse of Hatshepsut

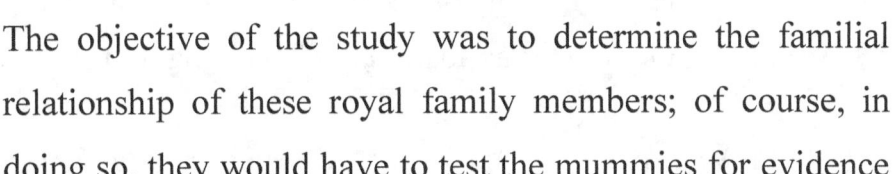

The objective of the study was to determine the familial relationship of these royal family members; of course, in doing so, they would have to test the mummies for evidence of murder, genetic disorders, and infectious diseases. [217]

Unlike the previous hypotheses about Tutankhamun's death and medical history, this investigation was based on unfettered access to the actual mummies. [218]

Using partial Y-chromosomal information, Hawass et al were able to construct the most plausible 5-generation pedigree to date, whereby ......

---

[217]

http://jama.jamanetwork.com/article.aspx?articleid=185374
[218] Ibid.

[1] Yuya (KV46) and Thuya (KV46) have been established as the parents of KV35 Elder Lady (Queen Tiye), making them great grandparents of Tutankhamun

[2] Pharaoh Amenhotep III (KV35) and KV35 Elder Lady (Queen Tiye) have been established as parents of both the KV55 male (most likely Akhenaten) and the KV35 Younger Lady, making them the grandparents of Tutankhamun

[3] the KV55 male (most likely Akhenaten) and KV35 Younger Lady, as full siblings, have been established as both the children of Pharaoh Amenhotep III (KV35) and KV35 Elder Lady (Queen Tiye), making them the parents of Tutankhamun [219] [220] [221]

219

http://jama.jamanetwork.com/article.aspx?articleid=185374
220

http://jama.jamanetwork.com/data/Journals/JAMA/4500/JWE05009_02_17_2010.pdf
221 http://www.drhawass.com/blog/press-release-discovery-family-secrets-king-tutankhamun

In addition, while Tutankhamun (KV62) might be the father of the fetuses also found in KV62, more data on the female mummies, KV21A and KV21B, are needed to confirm (finalize) this relationship. [222]

While the data obtained from KV21A *suggests* that she is the mother of the fetuses, the mother has not yet been genetically identified. [223]

As well, it is not yet statistically significant to be able to define her as Ankhensenamun. [224]

---

[222]

http://jama.jamanetwork.com/data/Journals/JAMA/4500/JWE05009_02_17_2010.pdf
[223]

http://jama.jamanetwork.com/article.aspx?articleid=185393
[224] Ibid.

The Merovingian Dynasty

▶Meroveus (Mérovée) [225] is attributed to being the progenitor of the Merovingian dynasty. Evidently, there was something special about King Meroveus and his priestly successors; not only were they accorded special veneration, but they were also widely known for their esoteric knowledge and occult skills.

This learned dynasty emerged in the ancient Nazarite tradition to become known as the long-haired Sorceror Kings. Noted sorcerors in the manner of the Samaritan Magi, they firmly believed in the hidden powers of the honeycomb, considered by philosophers to be the manifestation of divine harmony in nature because it is naturally made up of hexagonal prisms.

To the Merovingians, the bee was a most hallowed creature, having been a sacred emblem of Egyptian royalty.

---

[225] http://fmg.ac/Projects/MedLands/MEROVINGIANS.htm

Likewise, they believed it to be a symbol of wisdom.

The Merovingians were not a line of created kings, but those of natural descent.

Knowing their birthright, they based this natural selection and methods of ruling (by example and good works) upon King Solomon, their ancestor.

It is said that Mérovée was supposedly conceived when his mother, the wife of the king, encountered a Quinotaur (a sea monster that has the ability to change shape) while swimming.

I prefer to think along the lines of a foreign conqueror, coming from the sea, taking the dead king's wife (already pregnant) as his own (thereby impregnating her once again) in order to legitimize his claim.

►Childeric I [226] + Queen Basina of the Thuringians [227]

226

http://fmg.ac/Projects/MedLands/MEROVINGIANS.htm#C hildericdied481

Ad Infinitum: Unchanging and Forevermore

On May 27, 1653, a deaf-mute mason, named Adrien Quin-quin, was working on a construction project near the church of Saint-Brice in Tournai, Belgium.

According to Abbé Cochet, he was down about 7 or 8 feet when a blow of the pick revealed a gold buckle and at least a hundred gold coins.

This surprise find caused him to throw down the tool and run about, waving his arms and trying to articulate sounds.

The first witnesses "who crowded around the trench saw some two hundred silver coins; human bones, including two skulls; a lot of rusted iron; a sword with a gold grip and a hilt ornamented in the gold-and-garnet cloisonné technique and sheathed in a cloisonné decorated scabbard; and numerous other gold items, among them, brooches, buckles,

---

227

http://fmg.ac/Projects/MedLands/THURINGIA.htm#Basinus

rings, an ornament in the form of a bull's head, and about three hundred gold cloisonné bees." [228] [229] [230]

News of this treasure soon reached the archduke Leopold William, governor of the Austrian Netherlands, who had it sent to him in Brussels. It was he who further ordered that a carefully written account of the find be made, confiding the collection for study to his personal physician, Jean-Jacques Chifflet, who was also a historian.

---

[228]

http://content.yudu.com/Library/A18h8c/AncientEurope800 0BCt/resources/496.htm

[229] http://www.encyclopedia.com/article-1G2-3400400230/tomb-childeric.html

[230] http://gallica.bnf.fr/ark:/12148/btv1b7700172d

The outstanding find was a gold signet ring inscribed with the figure of an armed warrior and the name CHILDERICI REGIS.

It was this ring that identified the tomb as belonging to Childeric, the father of Clovis I. [231] [232]

---

[231]

http://en.wikipedia.org/wiki/File:CHILDERICI_REGIS.jpg
[232] http://courses.ttu.edu/jhowe/signet_ring.htm

In 1655, Jean-Jacques Chifflet published a folio volume of 367 pages with 27 plates of engravings furnishing an excellent visual record of all the artifacts and a careful discussion and interpretative essay identifying the subject as the father of Clovis I, the great ancestor of the French monarchy. [233]

Truly, this discovery is the starting point of Merovingian archaeology, and Chifflet's study deserves to be considered the first truly scientific archaeological publication. [234]

This study "has proved all the greater a boon because most of the original artifacts have disappeared. The archduke took them home to Vienna when he retired. Upon his death in 1662, they came into the possession of Leopold I,

---

[233] http://www.encyclopedia.com/article-1G2-3400400230/tomb-childeric.html
[234] Ibid.

emperor of Austria, who, in 1665, sent them to France as a diplomatic present to young King Louis XIV." [235]

The collection survived the French Revolution intact, but one night "in 1831 two thieves broke into the Bibliothèque Royal and stole the trove. By the time they were caught, most of the gold objects had been melted down, but a few artifacts, such as the gold cloisonné ornament of the sword, had been thrown into the Seine in leather sacks, and these were recovered." [236]

What do we honestly know about Childeric?

The sixth-century ecclesiastic and historian Gregory of Tours tells us something of his life in Historia Francorum (The History of the Franks). [237]

235

http://content.yudu.com/Library/A18h8c/AncientEurope800
0BCt/resources/498.htm
[236] Ibid.
[237] http://www.fordham.edu/halsall/basis/gregory-hist.asp

While Childeric may have been the son of Merovech, he was considered a king so debauched that his own subjects drove him into exile for eight years among the Thuringians, at the court of King Basinus and Queen Basina.

During this time the Roman general Aegidius ruled the Franks in his place. Upon his departure from court, Queen Basina followed him; they eventually married, and she gave birth to a son, Clovis.

Meanwhile Childeric fought a battle at Orléans against the Visigoths and another at Angers against the Goths and Saxons. When he died in about 481 AD, his son Clovis replaced him.

What continues to follow, herein, is my own line of descent.

► Clovis I [238] + St. Clothilde de Burgundy [239]

King of the Salian Franks (481 to 486 AD) as well as King of the Franks (486 to 511 AD), by age 20 he was a powerful leader, destined to become the most influential figure in the West.

He was the first King of the Franks to unite all the Frankish tribes under one ruler.

His wife, a Catholic, managed to convert him at a time when the entire Catholic Church was on the verge of collapse.

Word of his conversion soon spread and everyone in his realm began converting; had it not been to please his wife, the entire course of history in Europe would have been dramatically different, and Catholicism would probably have been relegated to some minor sect.

238

http://fmg.ac/Projects/MedLands/MEROVINGIANS.htm#_
Toc184188200
239

http://fmg.ac/Projects/MedLands/BURGUNDY%20KINGS.
htm#ChrotechildisOrClotildedied544

Instead, the Catholic bishops used this opportunity to maneuver the Merovingians strategically out of the picture.

King Clovis died in Paris at the age of 45.

His vast kingdom was divided among his four sons to rule, circa 511 AD: Clotaire I in Soissons, Childebert I in Paris, Chlodomer in Orléans, and Theuderic I in Rheims.

► Clotaire I [240] + Aregund von Thuringia [241]

King of Soissons (511 to 558 AD), King of Austrasia (555 to 558 AD) and King of the Franks (558 to 561 AD).

---

[240]

http://fmg.ac/Projects/MedLands/MEROVINGIANS.htm#ClotaireIdied561B

[241]

http://fmg.ac/Projects/MedLands/THURINGIA.htm#Radegunddied587

▶ Chilperic I [242] + Fredegund

King of Soissons (561 to 584 AD) and King of the Franks (567 to 584 AD).

▶ Clotaire II [243] + Haldetrude

King of Soissons (584 to 613 AD) and King of the Franks (613 to 628 AD).

▶ Dagobert I [244] + Nantilde (Nanthilda)

King of the Soissons (622 to 628 AD) and King of the Franks (628 to 639 AD).

---

[242]

http://fmg.ac/Projects/MedLands/MEROVINGIANS.htm#C hilpericIdied584B

[243]

http://fmg.ac/Projects/MedLands/MEROVINGIANS.htm#C lotaireIIdied629B

[244]

http://fmg.ac/Projects/MedLands/MEROVINGIANS.htm#D agobertIdied638B

►Clovis II [245] + Bathilde (Batilde) de France

King of Nestria and Burgundy (639 to 655 AD).

►Thierry (Theuderic) III [246] + Clotilde dite Doda

King of Nestria and Burgundy (675 AD) and King of Austrasia (675 to 691 AD).

►Bertrada of Prüm [247] [248] + unknown [249]

---

[245]

http://fmg.ac/Projects/MedLands/MEROVINGIANS.htm#ClovisIIdied657B

[246]

http://fmg.ac/Projects/MedLands/MEROVINGIANS.htm#TheodericIIIdied691

[247]

http://fmg.ac/Projects/MedLands/MEROVINGIANS.htm#TheodericIIIdied691

[248]

http://fmg.ac/Projects/MedLands/FRANKSMaiordomi.htm#_Toc284006018

[249] Posited as possibly being Norbert d'Aquitaine, son of Hugobert d'Aquitaine and d'Irmine d'Oeren, courtesy of http://nobles-ancetres.pagesperso-orange.fr/Familles/Hugobert.pdf

Bertrada founded Prüm Abbey, situated northwest of Trier, in 721 AD.

In 1975, another genealogy took into account three arguments that were proposed, all in keeping with Bertrada being the daughter of Thierry III and Clotilde dite Doda (meaning, that so, too, was she the sister of both Clovis IV and Clotaire IV). This argument also presumes that Doda, herself, is the daughter of Ansegisel and Begga, as well as the granddaughter of St. Arnulf and St. Dode. [250]

- Fact 1: Bertrada's husband is anonymous, and related to the Hugobertides. [251]
- Fact 2: As the daughter of Thierry III, Bertrada is Merovingian.
- Fact 3: The properties of Rommersheim and Rumbach were shared between Pépin of Herstal (who transferred his shares to Charles Martel), and Doda (who transmitted her shares to Bertrada).

---

[250] Settipani, Christian. (1989) Les ancêtres de Charlemagne. Paris, France: Société atlantique d'impression.
[251] http://fr.wikipedia.org/wiki/Hugobertides

Christian Settipani argues, on the basis of onomastics and the inheritance of the villa of Rommersheim, that Bertrada of Prüm was daughter of Théodéric III, stating that … "King Theoderic III had a wife Doda. This Doda could have been a daughter of Ansegisel, son of another Doda. Ansegisel, presumably, shares Rommersheim between his son, Pippin of Herstal and his daughter Doda, King Theoderic's wife. Then Pippin's son, Charles Martel inherits Rommersheim, and likewise, Bertrada, Doda's daughter. This explains why King Clothar IV, son of Theoderic III, was called the cousin of Charles Martel in the Adémar of Chabannes chronicle" (November 16, 1999 posting on Gen-Medieval-L). [252] [253] [254]

In addition, Hans J.C. Schats supports this line as a likely possibility in "Voorouders van Karel de Grote." [255] When

---

252

https://groups.google.com/forum/?fromgroups#!topic/soc.genealogy.medieval/R393UJl9pds

[253] http://www.geni.com/people/Bertrade-de-Pr%C3%BCm/6000000001842551452

254

http://en.wikipedia.org/wiki/The_Chronicon_of_Ademar_of_Chabannes

[255] http://www.kareldegrote.nl/

Bertrada donated land to the abbey of Prüm, the donation document was co-signed by her son Caribert and three witnesses, supposed to be her relatives, with the typical Merovingian names Bernier, Rolande and Thierry.

▶ Count Charibert de Laon [256] + unknown [257]

▶ Bertrada de Laon [258] [259] + Pépin III (Duke of Brabant) The Short [260]

King of the Franks (751 to 768 AD)

256

http://fmg.ac/Projects/MedLands/FRANKSMaiordomi.htm#_Toc284006018

[257] Posited as possibly being Bertrade de Cologne, daughter of Hugobert de Cologne et de Irmina d'Oeren, courtesy of http://nobles-ancetres.pagesperso-orange.fr/Familles/Hugobert.pdf

258

http://fmg.ac/Projects/MedLands/FRANKSMaiordomi.htm#Bertradadied783

[259] http://nobles-ancetres.pagesperso-orange.fr/Familles/Hugobert.pdf

260

http://fmg.ac/Projects/MedLands/CAROLINGIANS.htm#PepinleBrefFranksB

Pépin the Short, son of Charles Martel, in league with the Pope, was the first <u>coronated</u> king, deposing Childeric III, the next rightful successor of the Merovingian line; thus began the line of Kings known as the Carolingians.

► Charlemagne [261] [262] (Charles I) + Hildegard [263]

► Carloman, renamed Pépin I [264] [265] (King of Italy) + unknown

► Bernard (illegitimate issue) [266] [267] (King of Italy) + Cunégonde of Laon

---

[261]

http://fmg.ac/Projects/MedLands/CAROLINGIANS.htm#CharlemagneB

[262] http://www.francogene.com/genealogie-quebec-genealogy/010/010413.php

[263]

http://fmg.ac/Projects/MedLands/SWABIAN%20NOBILITY.htm#Hildegardisdied783

[264]

http://fmg.ac/Projects/MedLands/ITALY,%20Kings%20to%20962.htm#PepinIItalyB

[265] http://www.francogene.com/genealogie-quebec-genealogy/010/010412.php

▶Pépin II [268] [269] (Count of Vermandois) + unknown

▶Héribert I [270] [271] (Count of Vermandois) + unknown

▶Béatrice de Vermandois [272] [273] + Robert I (King of France) [274]

---

[266]

http://fmg.ac/Projects/MedLands/ITALY,%20Kings%20to%20962.htm#BernardIitalyB
[267] http://www.francogene.com/genealogie-quebec-genealogy/010/010411.php
[268]

http://fmg.ac/Projects/MedLands/FRANKISH%20NOBILITY.htm#Pepindiedafter850B
[269] http://www.francogene.com/genealogie-quebec-genealogy/010/010410.php
[270]

http://fmg.ac/Projects/MedLands/NORTHERN%20FRANCE.htm#HeribertIdied900907
[271] http://www.francogene.com/genealogie-quebec-genealogy/010/010409.php
[272]

http://fmg.ac/Projects/MedLands/NORTHERN%20FRANCE.htm#Beatrixdied931
[273] http://www.francogene.com/genealogie-quebec-genealogy/010/010408.php

▶Hughes le Grand [275] [276] (Duke of France) + Hedwige de Saxe (of Saxony) [277]

▶Hughes Capet [278] [279] (first Capetian King of France) + Adélaide de Poitou [280]

▶Robert II [281] [282] (King of France) + Constance de Provence [283]

---

[274]

http://fmg.ac/Projects/MedLands/CAPET.htm#RobertIdied9
23B
[275]

http://fmg.ac/Projects/MedLands/CAPET.htm#Huguesdied9
56B
[276] http://www.francogene.com/genealogie-quebec-
genealogy/010/010407.php
[277]

http://fmg.ac/Projects/MedLands/GERMANY,%20Kings.ht
m#HedwigMHuguesRegentFrancedied956
[278]

http://fmg.ac/Projects/MedLands/CAPET.htm#HuguesCapet
died996B
[279] http://www.francogene.com/genealogie-quebec-
genealogy/010/010406.php
[280]

http://fmg.ac/Projects/MedLands/AQUITAINE.htm#Adelais
died1004

▶ Henri I [284] [285] (King of France) + Anne de Kiev [286]

▶ Philippe I [287] [288] (King of France) + Berthe de Holland [289]

---

[281]

http://fmg.ac/Projects/MedLands/CAPET.htm#RobertIIdied1031B

[282] http://www.francogene.com/genealogie-quebec-genealogy/010/010405.php

[283]

http://fmg.ac/Projects/MedLands/PROVENCE.htm#ConstanceArlesMRobertIIFrancedied1031

[284]

http://fmg.ac/Projects/MedLands/CAPET.htm#HenriIdied1060B

[285] http://www.francogene.com/genealogie-quebec-genealogy/010/010404.php

[286]

http://fmg.ac/Projects/MedLands/RUSSIA,%20Rurik.htm#AnnaIaroslavnadied1075

[287]

http://fmg.ac/Projects/MedLands/CAPET.htm#PhilippeIdied1108B

[288] http://www.francogene.com/genealogie-quebec-genealogy/010/010403.php

[289]

http://fmg.ac/Projects/MedLands/HOLLAND.htm#Berthadied1093

▶Louis VI [290] [291] (King of France) + Adélaide de Savoie (of Savoy) de Maurienne [292]

▶Louis VII [293] [294] (King of France) + Adèle de Blois de Champagne [295]

▶Philippe II Auguste [296] [297] (King of France) + Agnès d'Andechs de Méranie [298]

---

[290]

http://fmg.ac/Projects/MedLands/CAPET.htm#LouisVIdied 1137B

[291] http://www.francogene.com/genealogie-quebec-genealogy/010/010402.php

[292]

http://fmg.ac/Projects/MedLands/SAVOY.htm#Adelaidedied1154

[293]

http://fmg.ac/Projects/MedLands/CAPET.htm#LouisVIIdied 1180B

[294] http://www.francogene.com/genealogie-quebec-genealogy/010/010401.php

[295]

http://fmg.ac/Projects/MedLands/CENTRAL%20FRANCE.htm#AdeleBloisdied1206

[296]

http://fmg.ac/Projects/MedLands/CAPET.htm#PhilippeIIdied1223B

▶Princess Marie de France [299] [300] [301] + Henri I (Duke of Brabant) [302]

▶Élisabeth de Brabant [303] [304] [305] + Count Dietrich (Thierry) de Clèves [306]

---

[297] http://www.francogene.com/genealogie-quebec-genealogy/010/010373.php

[298] http://fmg.ac/Projects/MedLands/CARINTHIA.htm#AgnesMeranodied1201

[299] http://fmg.ac/Projects/MedLands/CAPET.htm#Mariedied1238

[300] http://www.francogene.com/genealogie-quebec-genealogy/010/010372.php

[301] René Jetté, John P. DuLong, Roland-Yves Gagné and Gail F. Moreau; article entitled "From Catherine Baillon to Charlemagne" located in American Canadian Genealogist (pages 190, 191, 192). Issue 82, Volume 25, Number 4, 1999.

[302] http://fmg.ac/Projects/MedLands/BRABANT,%20LOUVAIN.htm#HenriILotharingiaBrabantdied1235B

[303] http://fmg.ac/Projects/MedLands/BRABANT,%20LOUVAIN.htm#Elisabethdied1272

[304] http://www.francogene.com/genealogie-quebec-genealogy/010/010371.php

▶Mathilde de Clèves [307] [308] [309] + Gérard de Luxembourg [310]

▶Marguerite de Luxembourg [311] [312] [313] + Jean III de Ghis-telles (a knight) [314]

---

[305] René Jetté, John P. DuLong, Roland-Yves Gagné and Gail F. Moreau; article entitled "From Catherine Baillon to Charlemagne" located in American Canadian Genealogist (page 190). Issue 82, Volume 25, Number 4, 1999.
[306]

http://fmg.ac/Projects/MedLands/FRANCONIA%20(LOWER%20RHINE).htm#Dietrichdied1245
[307]

http://fmg.ac/Projects/MedLands/FRANCONIA%20(LOWER%20RHINE).htm#Mechtilddied1304
[308] http://www.francogene.com/genealogie-quebec-genealogy/010/010370.php
[309] René Jetté, John P. DuLong, Roland-Yves Gagné and Gail F. Moreau; article entitled "From Catherine Baillon to Charlemagne" located in American Canadian Genealogist (page 189). Issue 82, Volume 25, Number 4, 1999.
[310]

http://fmg.ac/Projects/MedLands/LIMBURG.htm#GerardDubuydied12981303
[311] Ibid.
[312] http://www.francogene.com/genealogie-quebec-genealogy/010/010369.php
[313] René Jetté, John P. DuLong, Roland-Yves Gagné and Gail F. Moreau; article entitled "From Catherine Baillon to

▶Jean VI de Ghistelles [315] [316] [317] + Marie de Haverskerke [318]

▶Roger de Ghistelles [319] [320] [321] + Marguerite de Dudzeele

▶Isabelle de Ghistelles [322] [323] [324] + Arnould VI de Gavre [325]

Charlemagne" located in American Canadian Genealogist (pages 188, 189). Issue 82, Volume 25, Number 4, 1999.
[314] http://racineshistoire.free.fr/LGN/PDF/Ghistelles.pdf (page 3)
[315] http://racineshistoire.free.fr/LGN/PDF/Ghistelles.pdf (page 4)
[316] http://www.francogene.com/genealogie-quebec-genealogy/010/010368.php
[317] René Jetté, John P. DuLong, Roland-Yves Gagné and Gail F. Moreau; article entitled "From Catherine Baillon to Charlemagne" located in American Canadian Genealogist (page 188). Issue 82, Volume 25, Number 4, 1999.
[318] http://racineshistoire.free.fr/LGN/PDF/Haverskerque.pdf (page 9)
[319] http://racineshistoire.free.fr/LGN/PDF/Ghistelles.pdf (page 8)
[320] http://www.francogene.com/genealogie-quebec-genealogy/010/010354.php
[321] René Jetté, John P. DuLong, Roland-Yves Gagné and Gail F. Moreau; article entitled "From Catherine Baillon to Charlemagne" located in American Canadian Genealogist (pages 185, 186, 187, 188). Issue 82, Volume 25, Number 4, 1999.

▶Catherine de Gavre d'Escornaix [326] [327] [328] + Guy I Le Bouteiller [329]

Following the death of Guy I Le Bouteiller, Catherine married Simon Morhier (a knight) c. 1440. [330] [331]

---

[322] http://racineshistoire.free.fr/LGN/PDF/Ghistelles.pdf (page 8)

[323] http://www.francogene.com/genealogie-quebec-genealogy/010/010343.php

[324] René Jetté, John P. DuLong, Roland-Yves Gagné and Gail F. Moreau; article entitled "From Catherine Baillon to Charlemagne" located in American Canadian Genealogist (page 185). Issue 82, Volume 25, Number 4, 1999.

[325] http://racineshistoire.free.fr/LGN/PDF/Gavre.pdf (page 9)

[326] http://racineshistoire.free.fr/LGN/PDF/Gavre.pdf (page 10)

[327] http://www.francogene.com/genealogie-quebec-genealogy/010/010336.php

[328] René Jetté, John P. DuLong, Roland-Yves Gagné and Gail F. Moreau; article entitled "From Catherine Baillon to Charlemagne" located in American Canadian Genealogist (pages 183, 184). Issue 82, Volume 25, Number 4, 1999.

[329] http://racineshistoire.free.fr/LGN/PDF/Senlis.pdf (page 15)

[330] http://racineshistoire.free.fr/LGN/PDF/Gavre.pdf (page 10)

▶Guy II Le Bouteiller (a knight) [332] [333] [334] + Isabeau Morhier [335]

Isabeau was the daughter of Simon Morhier and Catherine de Gavre d'Escornaix. [336]

▶Jean Le Bouteiller [337] [338] [339] + Marie de Venois

---

[331] René Jetté, John P. DuLong, Roland-Yves Gagné and Gail F. Moreau; article entitled "From Catherine Baillon to Charlemagne" located in American Canadian Genealogist (page 182). Issue 82, Volume 25, Number 4, 1999.
[332] http://racineshistoire.free.fr/LGN/PDF/Senlis.pdf (page 15)
[333] http://www.francogene.com/genealogie-quebec-genealogy/010/010331.php
[334] René Jetté, John P. DuLong, Roland-Yves Gagné and Gail F. Moreau; article entitled "From Catherine Baillon to Charlemagne" located in American Canadian Genealogist (pages 182, 183). Issue 82, Volume 25, Number 4, 1999.
[335] http://racineshistoire.free.fr/LGN/PDF/Morhier.pdf (page 4)
[336] http://racineshistoire.free.fr/LGN/PDF/Morhier.pdf (page 4)
[337] http://racineshistoire.free.fr/LGN/PDF/Senlis.pdf (page 15)
[338] http://www.francogene.com/genealogie-quebec-genealogy/010/010321.php

▶Bénigne Le Bouteiller [340] [341] [342] + Jacques Maillard

▶Miles Maillard [343] [344] + Marie Morant

▶Renée Maillard [345] [346] + Adam Baillon

---

[339] René Jetté, John P. DuLong, Roland-Yves Gagné and Gail F. Moreau; article entitled "From Catherine Baillon to Charlemagne" located in <u>American Canadian Genealogist</u> (pages 179, 180, 181). Issue 82, Volume 25, Number 4, 1999.

[340] http://racineshistoire.free.fr/LGN/PDF/Senlis.pdf (page 15)

[341] http://www.francogene.com/genealogie-quebec-genealogy/010/010312.php

[342] René Jetté, John P. DuLong, Roland-Yves Gagné and Gail F. Moreau; article entitled "From Catherine Baillon to Charlemagne" located in <u>American Canadian Genealogist</u> (page 178). Issue 82, Volume 25, Number 4, 1999.

[343] http://www.francogene.com/genealogie-quebec-genealogy/010/010307.php

[344] René Jetté, John P. DuLong, Roland-Yves Gagné and Gail F. Moreau; article entitled "From Catherine Baillon to Charlemagne" located in <u>American Canadian Genealogist</u> (pages 177, 178). Issue 82, Volume 25, Number 4, 1999.

[345] http://www.francogene.com/genealogie-quebec-genealogy/010/010304.php

[346] René Jetté, John P. DuLong, Roland-Yves Gagné and Gail F. Moreau; article entitled "From Catherine Baillon to

▶Alphonse Baillon [347] [348] + Louise de Marle

▶Catherine Baillon [349] [350] + Jacques Miville dit Deschênes

Catherine was a *Fille du Roi*. Accordingly, Catherine, being from a family directly connected to minor French nobility, carried a dowry of 950 livres plus 50 livres from the King of France.

Catherine de Baillon was my 9th great grandmother.

Charlemagne" located in <u>American Canadian Genealogist</u> (page 177). Issue 82, Volume 25, Number 4, 1999.

[347] http://www.francogene.com/genealogie-quebec-genealogy/003/003676.php

[348] René Jetté, John P. DuLong, Roland-Yves Gagné and Gail F. Moreau; article entitled "From Catherine Baillon to Charlemagne" located in <u>American Canadian Genealogist</u> (pages 176, 177). Issue 82, Volume 25, Number 4, 1999.

[349] http://www.francogene.com/genealogie-quebec-genealogy/001/001079.php

[350] René Jetté, John P. DuLong, Roland-Yves Gagné and Gail F. Moreau; article entitled "From Catherine Baillon to Charlemagne" located in <u>American Canadian Genealogist</u> (pages 175, 176). Issue 82, Volume 25, Number 4, 1999.

Camelot

King Arthur, his knights, and all the inhabitants of Camelot believed in certain basic guiding principles.

The common man had rights, just as the noble did; women were respected, not used; a man's word was his honor; and people fought for those things because they believed in them, not because they were forced to by an overlord. [351]

By the same token, it is as equally important to acknowledge the truthfulness in knowing one's failings and limitations.

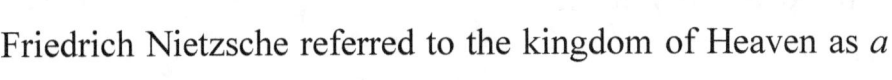

Friedrich Nietzsche referred to the kingdom of Heaven as *a condition of the heart*.

Does not this mean that love is the way to the kingdom that all are seeking?

---

[351] http://camelot.polestar.org/the_road.html

I see the Camelot, of Arthurian legend, as having been a state of mind (a spiritual kingdom) wherein the religion of the kingdom was none other than love.

When the two become as one, therein shall you find the true Holy Grail.

What does this mean? Is it deliberately meant to be cryptic in nature? Is it meant only for those who have eyes to see and ears to hear?

Every individual is on a journey of self; a journey of rediscovery, if you will.

In the integration of the dualistic parts of the self (light and dark, love and hate, masculine and feminine), we are able to revert back to our truest nature: one of compassion and compassionate allowing.

It shall be in this rediscovering of our true selves that we will have found the Holy Grail.

While the Holy Grail is the same for everyone, the process and experience(s) for each individual shall be vastly different; hence, we *all* become the Grail.

In having identified that there is something great at work, every time you are at peace, so, too, are you enlightened.

Inner peace is probably the most important thing that can be attained; when you experience inner peace, you are truly happy and content with your self. Your state of mind is a quiet mind and you are completely connected to God/dess.

God/dess and peace are synonymous. Inner turmoil is what suffocates your spirit, thereby preventing you from living from your higher self, unable to see life with a greater sense of clarity.

Enlightenment (the Holy Grail) is a state of being whereby you are reunited with your true spiritual self.

It is this connectedness, this freedom of self, that leads us to the ultimate and definitive realization that we are all one, thus imbuing our bodies with a sense of inner peace that allows us to joyfully accept and live life as per our creation.

We must take the time to revisit the message that Yeshua ben Yosef (Jesus) attempted to share with us 2,000 years ago, as opposed to that which has been corrupted, hijacked, fabricated and manufactured in his name, for therein lies the necessary truth(s).

Seek ye knowledge and ye shall find the truth that liberates. Seek ye discipline in the persisting with positive thoughts. Seek ye the joy of creating, the joy of learning, the joy of experiencing. Seek ye the realm of infinite possibilities for therein ye shall find the all. Seek ye the seer that ye be. [352]

---

[352] Doucette, Michele. (2010) <u>Veracity At Its Best</u> (page 142). McMinnville, TN: St. Clair Publications.

Preseli Bluestone

Preseli Bluestone is a type of Dolerite found only in the Preseli Mountains of Pembrokeshire in West Wales. [353] Most comes from a specific 3 km slope on Carn Menyn.

With an age of 480 million years, its primary composition being that of Calcium Feldspar and Augite, it is also known to contain Pyrite and traces of Copper. [354]

Some 4,500 years ago, the Neolithic Peoples, of what is now Britain, transported nineteen heavy pieces of Preseli Bluestone a distance of 150 miles to the Wiltshire Salisbury Plain. [355]

353

http://en.wikipedia.org/wiki/File:Carn_Menyn_bluestones_-_geograph.org.uk_-_1451509.jpg

[354] http://www.spiritualinspiration.org/t3321-preseli-bluestone

[355] Ibid.

If this feat alone was not awe inspiring enough, a further twenty-five to twenty-seven pieces were transported to the banks of the River Avon, to the West of Stonehenge, to form the recently discovered Bluestonehenge. [356]

Six years of excavation at Preseli have revealed settlements as old as 4,000 years before Stonehenge; burials also suggest visitors from far afield. [357]

The hills are peppered with holy wells, most of them spilling over pieces of the Dolerite Bluestone placed at their mouths, some carrying carved decoration; this stone, unique to the Preseli area, was clearly special. [358] Throughout history, holy wells and springs were regarded as curative, usually due to the water containing trace elements of minerals such as chalk, sulphur or iron. [359]

---

[356] http://www.spiritualinspiration.org/t3321-preseli-bluestone
[357] Ibid.
[358] Ibid.
[359] Ibid.

The many wells and springs at Preseli appear to go back long before the Bluestones arrived at Stonehenge, further suggesting that the wells and their Bluestones were already famed far and wide. [360]

Some of the enigma surrounding Stonehenge begins to fall in place with this view; especially the crippled Amesbury archer, and his son, who originated from the Alps, and then Kent, perhaps in desperate search of a cure for the dental abscess and osteoarthritis he is now known to have suffered from. [361]

With a reputation as a centre of healing, Stonehenge must have been well known, both locally and further afield, explaining to some degree its breath-taking architecture as well as the finds that were discovered from excavations two miles away at Durrington Walls; a Neolithic City of some

---

[360] http://www.spiritualinspiration.org/t3321-preseli-bluestone
[361] Ibid.

300 houses, making it *the largest neolithic settlement in northern Europe.* [362]

What has yet to be solved conclusively is the most intriguing mystery of all: why bring stones all the way from West Wales?

With these Bluestones forming part of a stone circle of larger sarsen sandstone blocks, once constructed, the acoustics of this structure was excellent for conducting ritual sound, most notably that of drums, long since used in meditative and shamanic practices. [363]

Preseli Bluestone contains a very powerful Earth Energy that has an anchoring effect on those who come into contact with it.

---

[362] http://www.spiritualinspiration.org/t3321-preseli-bluestone
[363] Ibid.

In more Modern times, Preseli Bluestone has been used to induce states of deep calm.

According to the online March 14, 2013 issue of *Maclean's* magazine, "the great mystery of Stonehenge appears to have been solved, and it is not an ancient astronomical tool. New research suggests Stonehenge marks a burial ground for elite families dating back to 3,000 BCE. Analysis of a nearby settlement also reveals that thousands of people, almost a tenth the entire population of Britain at the time, once descended on the site, in southwestern England, for communal celebrations." [364]

Bluestonehenge [365] [366]

---

[364] http://www2.macleans.ca/2013/03/14/good-news-22/

[365] http://en.wikipedia.org/wiki/Bluestonehenge

366

http://archive.archaeology.org/1001/trenches/bluestoneheng e.html

Bluestonehenge: An Ancient Alignment Revealed [367]

Blue Stonehenge Discovered [368]

Blue Stonehenge Discovered On The Banks of the River Avon [369]

Preseli Bluestone [370]

Preseli Bluestone Limited (featuring awesome jewelry) [371]

Preseli Bluestone Healing Information [372]

---

[367] http://en.wikipedia.org/wiki/Bluestonehenge
[368]

http://www.manchester.ac.uk/aboutus/news/display/?id=5111

[369] http://voices.yahoo.com/blue-stonehenge-discovered-banks-river-4607199.html?cat=8

[370] http://www.preselibluestone.net/

[371] http://www.stonehengestones.com/

[372]

http://www.preselibluestone.net/uploads/preselibluestone.pdf

Second Stonehenge Discovered Near Original [373]

Stonehenge [374]

Stonehenge and Bluestonehenge [375]

The Bluestonehenge Reconstruction (II) [376]

The Preseli Hills: An Historic Viewpoint [377]

---

[373] http://www.guardian.co.uk/science/2009/oct/06/second-stonehenge-discovered
[374] http://en.wikipedia.org/wiki/Stonehenge
[375]
http://www.youtube.com/playlist?list=PLA6A14FB4AAA4 6AFE
[376] http://digitaldigging.net/blog/the-bluestonehenge-reconstruction-ii/
[377] http://www.preselibluestone.net/uploads/History.pdf

Montségur

In the words of Saint Bernard of Clairveaux, the Cathars were described thusly ......

If you interrogate them, no one could be more Christian. As to their conversation, nothing can be less reprehensible, and what they speak, they prove by deeds. As for the morals of the heretics, they cheat no one, they oppress no one, they strike no one. [378]

From 1208 to 1244 the first European holocaust was conducted.

---

[378] Freke, Timothy, and Gandy, Peter. (2001) Jesus and The Lost Goddess: The Secret Teachings of the Original Christians (page 84). Three Rivers Press: New York, New York.

The Church of Rome (later known as the Roman Catholic Church) savagely attacked the Cathars of Southern France; they attacked with a viciousness that would later show itself paralleled in the atrocities committed, against the Jews, during World War II.

The Cathars claimed to possess a secret <u>Book of Love</u>, a gospel of Jesus (Yeshua), written not in words, but in symbols derived from a very ancient tradition; a book that was given to John the Divine.

The existence of this lost (or hidden) gospel, the foundation of the Cathar Church of Love (or Amor, the total reversal of Roma, meaning Rome), was revealed when the Church subjected the Cathars to torture; likewise, during the torturing of the Templar Knights in 1308.

The Cathars, aware of the laws of Duality, were adepts at the transmutation of darkness through love and purity.

Man participates in God's victory toward ignorance (the absence of Light) and evil (absence of Love); the Cathars taught internal alchemy, which is the transmutation of the physical self into Gold (Golden Light). [379]

The contents of the <u>Book of Love</u> involved a secret skill (symbolized by the Templar skull) said to both grant one the ability to control the forces of nature as well as to transform human blood into that of the wise, holy and pure blood of life equated with the Holy Grail. The point was to know the Grail, not as a cup, but as a transformation process from homo sapien into a pure one.

Below Montségur lies a peaceful meadow, its name *Prat dels Cremats* meaning *the Field of the Burnt Ones*, the only indication of a grim event that took place on March 16, 1244, when two hundred and five Cathars were burned alive on this very site, rather than denounce their creed.

---

[379] http://erzengelmichael.org/Erzengel-Mi-chael/Gottlicher_Plan/Eintrage/2012/5/1_The_Cathars.html

I herein thank Rolf Müller, for granting me the privilege of using his photograph, Cathar Dove, a close-up feature on the monument to the Cathars, located in Minerve, France.

You may view his online Flickr photostream at http://www.flickr.com/photos/gripspix/

One of the few known surviving Cathar artifacts (stone dove) to be recovered from Montségur, it is now housed in a private collection in Toulouse.

http://www.russianbooks.org/montsegur/montsegur1.htm

Cathar coin found at Montségur

http://www.bibliotecapleyades.net/imagenes_cataros/catar_c
oin.jpg

House of Bourbon

The House of Bourbon is a European royal house of French origin, a branch of the Capetian dynasty. Bourbon kings first ruled Navarre, originally the kingdom of Pamplona, one that occupied lands on either side of the Pyrenees, alongside the Atlantic Ocean between present day Spain and France, from 1555, and France, from 1589, until the 1792 overthrow of the monarchy during the French Revolution.

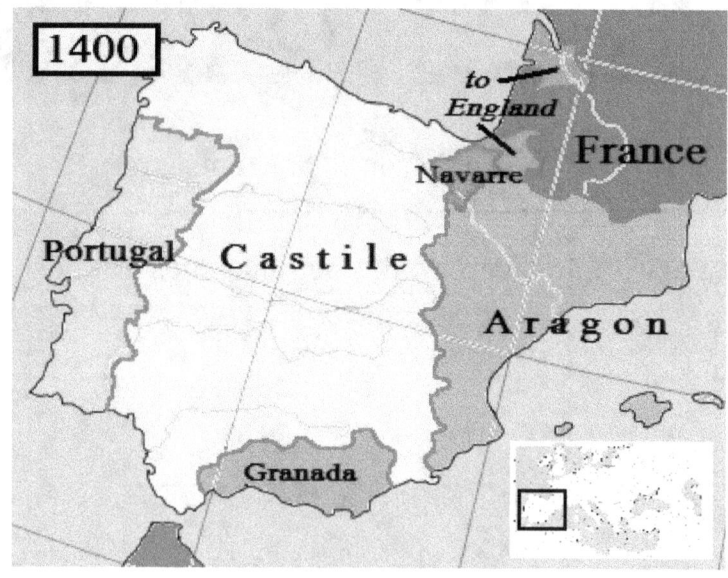

http://en.wikipedia.org/wiki/File:Navarre1400.png

By the 18th century, members of the Bourbon dynasty also held thrones in Spain, Naples, Sicily and Parma. Currently, both Spain and Luxembourg have Bourbon monarchs.

Henri IV of France, head of the House of Bourbon, became the senior Capet, following the extinction of the male line of the House of Valois. All members of the House of Bourbon, and its cadet branches alive today, are direct descendants of Henri IV.

The following table represents my familial connection to Henri IV of France (also Henri III, King of Navarre).

Many of these connections can also be found in my maternal genealogy volumes: [1] Men and Women of Renown: My Maternal Genealogy and [2] Men and Women of Renown: The Companion Volume.

Robert of Hesbaye	Robert of Hesbaye
Robert III, Count of Worms and Rheingau	Robert III, Count of Worms and Rheingau
Robert the Strong, Duke of France	Robert the Strong, Duke of France
King Robert I of France	King Robert I of France
Hugues the Great, Duke of France	Hugues the Great, Duke of France

King Hugues Capet of France	King Hugues Capet of France
King Robert II of France	King Robert II of France
King Henri I of France	King Henri I of France
King Philippe I of France	King Philippe I of France
King Louis VI of France	King Louis VI of France
King Louis VII of France	King Louis VII of France
King Philippe II Auguste of France	**King Philippe II Auguste of France**
King Louis VIII of France	Princess Marie of France
King Louis IX of France	Élisabeth de Brabant
Robert, Count of Clermont	Mathilda de Clèves
Louis I, Duke of Bourbon	Marguerite de Luxembourg
James I, Count of La Marche	Jean IV de Ghistelles
Jean I, Count of La Marche	Roger de Ghistelles
Louis I, Count of Vendôme	Isabelle (Ysabeau) de Ghistelles
Jean VIII, Count of Vendôme	Catherine de Gavre d'Escornaix
François, Count of Vendôme	Guy II Le Bouteillier
Charles, Duke of Vendôme	Jean Le Bouteillier
Antoine of Navarre, Duke of Vendôme	Bénigne Le Bouteillier
Henri III, King of Navarre Henri IV of France	Miles Maillard
	Renée Maillard
	Alphonse de Baillon
	Catherine de Baillon, my 9th great grandmother, a *Fille du Roi* of minor French nobility

Until I began to undertake research for this book, I would never have suspected that I was related to Henri IV of France, a Huguenot.

Baptised as a Catholic, his mother, Jeanne d'Albret, Queen of Navarre, had been raised in the Protestant tradition.

Upon the death of his mother, he inherited the throne of Navarre in 1572. It had also been arranged that Henri would marry Marguerite de Valois, a royal Princess, the last of the house of Valois; they were wed, in Paris, on August 18, 1572.

On August 24, 1572, the Saint Bartholomew's Day Massacre began; several thousand Huguenot Protestants who had come to Paris for Henri's wedding were killed, as well as thousands more throughout the country in the days that followed.

With both the help of his wife, as well as his promise to her that he would convert to Catholicism, Henri narrowly escapes death.

As leader of the Huguenots, it was at the urging of his faithful friend, Théodore Agrippa d'Aubigné, that he fled the court of France in 1576. Having abjured Catholicism at Tours, he quickly rejoined the Protestant forces in the military conflict.

Henri's first wife, Marguerite de Valois, was famous for her beauty and sense of style; one of the most fashionable women of her time, she was quick to influence many of the royal courts of Europe with the style of clothing that she wore.

Whilst court living was one of refinement, and one that Marguerite religiously adhered to, she found the habits of her nineteen year old husband to be quite backward and socially incompatible.

Abhorrently repulsed by her husband, Marguerite took many lovers, both during her marriage and after her annulment.

Completely indifferent to his wife, Henri also engaged in numerous infidelities.

After Henri fled in 1576, Marguerite was granted permission to return to her husband in Navarre. Over the duration of three and a half years, they lived in Pau; both openly kept other lovers, and they quarreled frequently.

After an illness in 1582, Marguerite returned to the court of her brother, Henri III, in Paris; scandalized by her reputation, she was soon forced to leave.

After long negotiations, she was allowed to return to her husband's court in Navarre, but to a most standoffish reception.

Having masterminded a coup d'état, she seized power over the city of Agen. After several months of fortifying the city, the citizens revolted, leaving Marguerite naught but to flee to the castle of Carlat.

In 1586, she was imprisoned in the castle of Usson, in Auvergne, by her brother Henri III; it was here that she spent eighteen years.

By 1589, upon the death of Henri III of France, Henri III of Navarre had succeeded to the throne of France as Henri IV.

Not accepted by most of the Catholic population, he converted four years later.

Negotiations to annul the marriage began in 1592 and were concluded in 1599 with an agreement that allowed Marguerite to maintain the title of queen.

It was following the annulment of this marriage that Henri married Marie de Medici in October 1600.

In 1557, the name Nicolaus Mius of Grÿnn appears on the register of the University of Orléans, one of five German students. [380]

http://mius-dentremont-dna-project.tripod.com/miusdentremontdnaproject

---

[380] http://doris_muise.tripod.com/muise2.htm

It reads *D Nicolaus Mius a Grÿnn*.

The D stands for *Dominus* which is Latin for Mister, and Grÿnn, which follows, indicates where he came from.

By 1569, Nicolaus was married to Jeanne, surname unknown; they had several children.

It is this same Nicolaus (Nicolas) Mius who was the chamber valet of Admiral Gaspard de Coligny II, the French Huguenot leader.

Admiral Gaspard II de Coligny

http://en.wikipedia.org/wiki/File:Fran%C3%A7ois_Clouet_-_Admiral_Gaspard_II_de_Coligny.jpg

In Admiral Gaspard de Coligny's will, Nicolaus is mentioned:

To Nicolas Mouche (Mius), my chamber valet and his wife, Jeanne, for their good services, to me and my wife, I give them five hundred francs in money one time and six septiers of bled metail (mixture of wheat and rye) the rest of their lives solely so they can have more children. [381]

Nicolaus also served as interpreter for Admiral Gaspard de Coligny, the military and political leader of the Huguenots. Both of these men were killed on August 24, 1572 during the St. Bartholomew's Day Massacre in Paris.

The slaughter of French Huguenots quickly spread to the provinces and about 20,000 Huguenots were ultimately killed by Roman Catholic mobs.

The prime responsibility for the massacre was borne by Catherine de Medici, who opposed the influence of the

---

[381] http://doris_muise.tripod.com/muise2.htm

Protestant leader, Admiral Gaspard II de Colignay, over her weak son, King Charles IX. [382]

Father Clarence d'Entremont, author of Histoire du Cap- Sable, read Grÿnn simply as Grynn. In searching for Grynn (minus the two dots above the y), the closest he could find was the village of Gryon located in the Canton of Vaud (Switzerland).

In a question posed to the Cantonales Vaudroises, in Lausanne, Switzerland, touching on the origin of Nicolas Mius, a response, dated September 13, 1978, shared that this family name did not appear in the region of Vaud, and specifically, not in Gryon; so, too, did it become known, in 2008, and validated, once again, in 2013, that Gryon was never called, or spelled, as either Grynn or Grÿnn. [383]

382

http://en.wikisource.org/wiki/Lectures_on_Modern_History/ The_Huguenots_and_the_League

[383] https://www.familytreedna.com/public/Mius-dEntremont

The dotted y, as found in Grÿnn, was apparently used often in place of a simple y. It is also used as a Dutch or Flemish ij, as in Grijnn, which looks like Grÿnn in cursive writing.

Neither Grijnn nor Grÿnn has been located on maps, both modern and 16th century, of Holland or Belgium.

While Grÿnn has not been found on modern maps of Germany, historical maps have yet to be investigated.

There was also another German student in attendance (at the University of Orléans) by the name of Conrad Maius; he could have been from the same family. [384]

The name, originally Majus, was often written as Maius. [385] In German, the letters ai are pronounced as i, thereby resulting in the present pronunciation Mius (my-us). [386]

---

[384] http://doris_muise.tripod.com/muise2.htm
[385] Ibid.
[386] Ibid.

Given that these times were significantly dangerous for Calvinist Protestants, could it be that Nicolaus Mius may have written a fictitious place name (Grÿnn) in the register of the University of Orléans in order to further protect his family?

Admiral Gaspard II de Coligny, Seigneur de Châtillon, had been married twice. [387]

His first wife, Charlotte de Laval, died on March 3, 1568. [388]

He was then married, a second time, to Countess Jacqueline d'Entremont of the House of Montbel d'Entremont of Savoie, in 1571. [389]

---

[387] http://en.wikipedia.org/wiki/Gaspard_II_de_Coligny
[388] http://en.wikipedia.org/wiki/Charlotte_de_Laval
[389]

http://fr.wikipedia.org/wiki/Jacqueline_de_Montbel_d'Entremont

Following the death of her husband, Countess Jacqueline (the only daughter and heiress of the Montbel d'Entremont family of Savoy), [390] a widow for the second time, felt indebted to the orphaned children of Nicolaus, taking a son (unfortunately there is no record of his first name) under her protection. [391]

In the marriage contract between the Admiral and Jacqueline, there is a clause that reads as follows: *The first originating from the marriage and his descendants, whether male or female, would carry the name and coat of arms of Count d'Entremont* (denoted by Jacqueline's father). [392]

Béatrice de Coligny, Countess d'Entremont, was born on December 21, 1572. [393]

390

http://fr.wikipedia.org/wiki/Jacqueline_de_Montbel_d'Entremont
[391] http://doris_muise.tripod.com/muise2.htm
[392] Ibid.
393

http://fr.wikipedia.org/wiki/Jacqueline_de_Montbel_d'Entremont

On November 30, 1600, she was married to Claude Antoine Bon, Baron of Meuillon and Montauban, Governor of Marseilles; and their first born, a son, was named François Virgine. [394] [395]

It has been further speculated that Claude Antoine Bon de Meuillon was the biological son of Nicolaus Mius (killed while defending the wounded Coligny), adopted by the Bon de Meuillon family of Marseilles. [396] [397]

Nicolas Mius also left two daughters, Charlotte Mousche and Louyse Mousche, both of whom were put in the care of Louise de Coligny, Princess of Orange, daughter of the Admiral and his first wife, widow of William of Nassau, Prince of Orange (dit *le Taciturne*). [398]

---

[394] http://michaelmarcotte.com/dentremontOrigin.htm
[395] http://genealogiequebec.info/images/20060221.pdf
[396] Ibid.
[397] http://michaelmarcotte.com/dentremontOrigin.htm
[398] http://doris_muise.tripod.com/muise2.htm

It is plausible that Philippe Mius d'Entremont, aka François Virgine, Count d'Entremont, could have deliberately hid his true identity, in Acadie, to avoid complications from past Huguenot related activities in France.

In 1651, it is known that Philippe Mius d'Entremont, his wife Madeleine Hélie, and their 4 year old daughter, Marguerite, sailed from La Rochelle, France, with Charles de Latour, and a number of his men, arriving in Acadie during the month of August. [399]

As denoted on the Mius d'Entremont Family Tree DNA project website, [400] *we are actively endeavoring to determine if, indeed, François Virgine d'Entremont and Philippe Mius d'Entremont were one and the same person; likewise, for the two wives of these two fellows, namely, Madeleine Élie du Tillet and Madeleine Hélie.*

---

[399] http://doris_muise.tripod.com/muise2.htm
[400] https://www.familytreedna.com/public/mius-dentremont/default.aspx

Ad Infinitum: Unchanging and Forevermore

Actes du Colloque l'Admiral de Coligny et son Temps [401]

A Little Controversy [402]

Ancestry of Philippe Mius d'Entremont [403]

Famille du Tillet [404]

François Virgine Bon, Comte d'Entremont et de Montbel [405]

La Généalogie (in French) [406]

La Généalogie (translation) [407]

---

[401] http://michaelmarcotte.com/MiusdEntremont.htm

[402] http://www.museeacadien.ca/argyle/html/egenealogy5.htm

[403] http://www.lagenealogy.net/Documents/dentremontOrigin.pdf

[404] http://racineshistoire.free.fr/LGN/PDF/du_Tillet.pdf (page 5)

[405] http://genealogiequebec.info/testphp/info.php?no=193963

[406] http://www.museeacadien.ca/argyle/html/fgenealogie4.htm

[407] http://translate.google.com/translate?hl=en&sl=fr&tl=en&u

Marcotte Genealogy: François Virgine Bon [408]

Marcotte Genealogy via Melancon [409]

Mius d'Entremont Family Tree DNA [410]

The Mius d'Entremont Controversy [411] [412]

The Nicolas Mius Story [413]

The Philippe Mius d'Entremont Story [414]

=http%3A%2F%2Fwww.museeacadien.ca%2Fargyle%2Fhtml%2Ffgenealogie4.htm

[408] http://michaelmarcotte.com/francoisebon.htm

[409] http://michaelmarcotte.com/melancon.htm

[410] https://www.familytreedna.com/public/mius-dentremont/default.aspx

[411] http://michaelmarcotte.com/dentremontOrigin.htm

[412] http://genealogiequebec.info/images/20060221.pdf

[413] http://doris_muise.tripod.com/muise2.htm

[414] http://www.lagenealogy.net/Pages/mius.aspx

Epilogue

Standing on the 21st century precipice of a spiritual revolution, like Akhenaton, so, too, are we being called upon to challenge the status quo, to challenge previously held beliefs, to seek the truth(s) that exist within, while also making use of personal discernment along the way.

As my friend, Ivan Fraser of <u>The Truth Campaign</u> shares ... *The bigger the lie, the more people will believe it. If you know the truth, then you cannot be taken in by the lie. However, if you believe lies, then all you will find is evidence to reinforce the illusion. The only solution is a truly open mind, a willingness to shed one's dogmas no matter how dearly cherished, and absolute honesty.*

The only question that bodes asking is ... are you ready?

Bibliography

AKHENATEN AND NEFERTITI

Although Ahmed Osman, David Rohl, and William Theaux each have evinced their own controversial theories, there is an uncanny synergy between them. The powerful insight gained through integrating their collective research would therefore ascribe far greater credence to their individual works. [415]

Ahmed Osman [416] [417] [418] [419] [420]

Akhenaten [421]

---

[415] http://www.domainofman.com/ankhemmaat/integrat.html
[416] http://ahmedosman.com/home.html
[417] http://freespace.virgin.net/a.osman/
[418] http://domainofman.com/ankhemmaat/osman.html
[419] http://dwij.org/forum/amarna/egypt_intro.html
[420] http://dwij.org/forum/amarna/egypt_articles.html
[421] http://www.heptune.com/Akhnaten.html

Akhenaten and Monotheism [422]

Akhenaten and Moses [423] [424]

Akhenaten and The Armana Period [425]

Akhenaten and The Religion of The Aten [426]

Akhenaten Trismegiste (William Theaux) [427]

Akhenaten versus Moses, Part 1 [428]

---

[422]
http://www.usu.edu/markdamen/1320Hist&Civ/chapters/10
AKHEN.htm
[423] http://www.egypt-tehuti.org/downloadarticles/akhenaton-
moses.pdf
[424] http://www.acacialand.com/Akhnaton.html
[425]
http://www.bbc.co.uk/history/ancient/egyptians/akhenaten_0
1.shtml
[426] http://www.osirisnet.net/docu/akhenat/e_akhen1.htm
[427]
http://www.smashwords.com/extreader/read/139951/1/akhe
naton-trismegiste
[428] http://tedloukes.blogspot.ca/2011/08/akhenaten-v-moses-
akhenaten.html

Akhenaten versus Moses, Part 2 [429]

Akhenaten versus Moses, Part 3 [430]

Akhenaten versus Moses, Part 4 [431]

Akhenaten versus Moses, Part 5 [432]

Amenhotep IV, Akhenaton and Moses [433]

An Analysis of the Pharaoh Akhenaten's Religious and Philosophical Revolution [434]

Ancient Egyptian Sexuality, Part 1 [435]

---

[429] http://tedloukes.blogspot.ca/2011/09/akhenaten-v-moses-moses.html
[430] http://tedloukes.blogspot.ca/2011/10/akhenaten-v-moses-joseph-and-yuya.html
[431] http://tedloukes.blogspot.ca/2011/10/long-live-horus-mighty-bull-who-rises.html
[432] http://tedloukes.blogspot.ca/2011/11/akhenaten-v-moses-part-5.html
[433] http://egyptianchristianity.com/akhenaton_moses.htm
[434] http://dl.tufts.edu/catalog/tufts:UA005.011.032.00001
[435] http://tiffanyweb.bmts.com/~damilos/sexuality.html

Ad Infinitum: Unchanging and Forevermore

Ancient Egyptian Sexuality, Part 2 [436]

Ancient Egypt's Crisis of Reason: Political, Theological and Phylogenetic Aspects of Akhenaten's Divine Kingship [437]

Ancient History Sourcebook: Egypt [438]

Armana Papers [439]

Atenism and Its Antecedents [440]

Blog of David Rohl [441]

Bust of Queen Nefertiti [442]

Coming of Age in Ancient Egypt [443]

[436] http://tiffanyweb.bmts.com/~damilos/sexuality2.html
[437] http://tiffanyweb.bmts.com/~damilos/dominantlogic.htm
[438] http://www.fordham.edu/Halsall/ancient/asbook04.asp
[439] http://tiffanyweb.bmts.com/~damilos/amarna.html
[440] http://www.ancient-egypt.co.uk/people/the-aten.htm
[441] http://davidrohlontour.blogspot.ca/
[442] http://www.egyptian-museum-berlin.com/c53.php
[443] http://tiffanyweb.bmts.com/~damilos/ComingofAge.htm

Did Akhenaten Influence Jewish Religion? [444]

DNA Shows That KV55 Mummy Probably Not Akhenaten [445]

Domain of Man (Charles Pope) [446]

Egypt 2012 [447]

Egypt Reveals Tutankhamun's Lineage [448]

Forgotten Origins [449]

Horemheb On The Wed (Daniel Kolos) [450]

Iona, Mystic Island [451]

---

[444] http://www.tektonics.org/copycat/akhenaten.php
[445] http://www.kv64.info/2010/03/dna-shows-that-kv55-mummy-probably-not.html
[446] http://www.domainofman.com/
[447] http://tedloukesegypt2012.blogspot.ca/
[448] http://news.xinhuanet.com/english2010/culture/2010-02/17/c_13178215.htm
[449] http://neros.lordbalto.com/
[450] http://www.horemheb.com/index.html
[451] http://herebedragons.weebly.com/iona-mystic-island.html

Ireland, Land of The Pharaohs (Andrew Power) [452]

Joseph and Akhenaten: The Case for Reinterpreting Amarna [453] [454]

King Tut's DNA Results: Was Akhenaten Joseph, Son of Jacob? [455]

King Tut Felled By Malaria, Bone Disease [456]

---

[452]

http://api.ning.com/files/rJGrnYss69reaTRACvXqV0ozSNb z7DOpM*ZPWyC77--6ztWWJxE- etqcKMQP69Jj*Qk*AOpq8nVl*3osCjCt9c- kcTvTmSA6/IRELANDLANDOFTHEPHAROA0HS.pdf

[453] http://www.unexplained- mysteries.com/forum/index.php?showtopic=235922&st=0

[454] http://mysite.verizon.net/joesniderman/Joseph%20and%20A khenaten.pdf

[455] http://ufodigest.ca/article/king-tuts-dna-results-was- akhenaten-joseph-son-jacob

[456] http://news.discovery.com/history/king-tut-dna- lineage.html

Moses and Akhenaten [457] [458] [459]

National Geographic Royal Relations [460]

Nefertiti: Partner in Akhenaten's Religious Revolution [461]

New Order of The Sun [462]

Queen Nefertiti [463]

Surest Signs of Piety [464]

The Akhenaten Temple Project [465]

---

[457]

http://www.grahamhancock.com/forum/osman_moses.php?p
=2

[458] http://esotericreader.com/2013/04/07/moses-and-
akhenaten-the-secret-history-of-egypt-at-the-time-of-the-
exodus/

[459] http://www.greatdreams.com/moses.htm

[460] http://ngm.nationalgeographic.com/2010/09/tut-dna/tut-
family-tree

[461] http://www.womenintheancientworld.com/nefertiti.htm

[462] http://www.savitridevi.org/article_eng_english.html

[463] http://www.touregypt.net/featurestories/nefertiti.htm

[464] http://www.domainofman.com/book/chap-16.html

[465] http://www.personal.psu.edu/users/d/b/dbr3/

Ad Infinitum: Unchanging and Forevermore

The Armana Period [466]

The Copper Scroll of Qumran [467]

The Dream Stela of Tuthmosis IV [468]

The Failed Reforms of Akhenaten and Muwatalli [469]

The Great Hymn to Aten [470] [471] [472] [473] [474] [475] [476] [477] [478] [479]

---

[466] http://www.touregypt.net/featurestories/amarnaperiod.htm
[467] http://www.bibliotecapleyades.net/mistic/scroll_qumran.htm
[468] http://www.pbs.org/wgbh/nova/ancient/sphinx-stela.html
[469] http://www.britishmuseum.org/pdf/6d%20The%20failed%20reforms.pdf
[470] http://www.digitalegypt.ucl.ac.uk/amarna/belief.html
[471] http://ecworlddynamics.wikispaces.com/file/view/Great+Hymn+to+the+Aten.pdf
[472] http://ashraf62.wordpress.com/2011/11/08/akhenatens-hymn-to-the-aten/
[473] http://www.seanet.com/~realistic/psalm104.html
[474] http://www.rostau.org.uk/aye/index.html
[475] http://historyarchaeology.wordpress.com/2013/05/21/the-great-hymn-to-the-aten/
[476] http://www.maat.sofiatopia.org/aten.htm

The Reforms of Akhenaten [480]

The Lost Pharaoh: The Search for Akhenaten [481]

The Moses Mystery [482]

The Quest for the Roots of the Judaic Monotheism in African Perspective [483]

477

http://supersededotcom.wordpress.com/2012/04/17/akhenatens-hymn-to-the-aten-similarities-in-the-attributes-and-praises-with-biblical-parallels-and-psalm-104-4/

478 http://www.dubiousdisciple.com/2013/04/psalm-104-the-great-hymn-to-the-aten-2.html

479

http://www.academia.edu/6076411/Atenism_and_The_Great_Hymn_to_the_Aten

480

http://www.theancientegyptians.com/ReformsAkhenaten.htm

481

https://www.nfb.ca/film/lost_pharaoh_search_for_akhenaten

482 http://fontes.lstc.edu/~rklein/Documents/mosesone.htm

483

http://www.gjournals.org/GJAH/GJAH%20PDF/2013/August/022013480%20Sangotunde.pdf

The Real Story of The Mysterious Queen Nefertiti [484]

Tutankhamun and Larger Foetus DNA [485]

Tutankhamun`s DNA Analysis [486]

Tutankhamun DNA Family Tree [487]

BRONZE SCULPTURE

Bronze Sculpture [488] [489]

From Digital Sculpting to Bronze Sculpture [490]

---

[484] http://www.youtube.com/watch?v=N0ZDDxeU4q0

[485] http://www.kv64.info/2010/06/tutankhamun-larger-foetus-dna.html

[486] http://www.unexplained-mysteries.com/forum/index.php?showtopic=175762&st=0

[487] http://www.kv64.info/2010/08/tutankhamun-dna-family-tree.html

[488] http://en.wikipedia.org/wiki/Bronze_sculpture

[489] http://popular.ebay.com/art/bronze-sculpture.htm

[490] http://www.cgpeoplenetwork.com/surprise/Lady-of-Naga-From-Digital-Sculpting-to-Bronze-Sculpture-000001733P/

How Bronze Sculpture Is Made [491]

How to Create and Cast Bronze Sculpture [492]

How to Make a Bronze Sculpture, Part 1 [493]

How to Make a Bronze Sculpture, Part 2 [494]

How to Make a Sculpture [495]

Sculpting in Bronze [496]

Sculpting in Clay for Bronze: The Process [497]

---

[491] http://www.collectorsguide.com/fa/fa023.shtml
[492] http://www.youtube.com/watch?v=W-g7zVcg1_4
[493]

http://playgallery.org/video/how_to_make_a_bronze_sculpt
ure_part_one/
[494]

http://playgallery.org/video/how_to_make_a_bronze_sculpt
ure_part_two/
[495] http://www.vanessa-pooley-bronze-sculptures.com/how-
to-make-a-sculpture.html
[496] http://www.bronzedreams.com/sculpting.html
[497] http://www.finearttips.com/2010/05/sculpting-in-clay-
for-bronze-the-process/

Sunti World Art [498]

The Story of Sculpture: From Clay to Bronze [499]

CATHARS AT MONTSÈGUR

A Survey of Recent Research on the Albigensian Cathari [500]

Cathar (Albigensian) and Baltic Crusades (1208 to 1300) [501]

Cathar Castles [502]

Catharism [503]

Catharism, Levitov and the Voynich Manuscript [504]

---

[498] http://www.suntiworldart.com/bronze-faq.html
[499] http://www.gobronze.org/from.html
[500]

http://www.jstor.org/discover/10.2307/3162901?uid=373941
6&uid=2&uid=3737720&uid=4&sid=21103653948811
[501] http://home.eckerd.edu/~oberhot/cathar.htm
[502] http://www.catharcastles.info/
[503] http://www.bbc.co.uk/programmes/p005488v
[504]

http://www.bibliotecapleyades.net/ciencia/esp_ciencia_man
uscrito04.htm

Cathar Martyrdom: The Cathar View [505]

Cathars and Cathar Beliefs in the Languedoc [506]

Cathars and Catharism [507]

Cathars and the Inquisition [508]

Catholics, Heretics and Heresy (Gilles Nullens) [509]

Château de Montségur [510] [511]

Consolamentum [512] [513] [514] [515] [516] [517]

505

http://www.dhaxem.com/data/handt/Cathar_Martyrdom.pdf
[506] http://www.castlesandmanorhouses.com/cathars/
[507] http://www.chemins-cathares.eu/index_uk.php
[508] http://www.san.beck.org/GPJ8-ManiandCathars.html#4
[509] http://www.nullens.org/catholics-heretics-and-heresy/#.U0loQMpOXyc
510

http://www.catharcastles.info/montsegur.php?key=montsegur
511

http://fr.wikipedia.org/wiki/Ch%C3%A2teau_de_Monts%C3%A9gur
[512] http://en.wikipedia.org/wiki/Consolamentum

Dhaxem: The Cathar Testament [518]

Faith of the Cathars [519]

Heretics [520]

Interrogatio Johannis [521]

In the Footsteps of the Cathars [522]

---

[513] http://gnosis.org/library/Consolamentum.html
[514] http://en.wikipedia.org/wiki/Catharism#Sacraments
[515] http://www.cathar.info/12011001_consolamentum.htm
[516] http://www.lectoriumrosicrucianum.org/artikel/the-history-of-the-cathars-part-3-of-3-the-occitan-consolamentum?page=0,1
[517] http://www.gnostic-jesus.com/gnostic-jesus/Medieval/Consolamentum.html
[518] http://www.dhaxem.com/
[519] http://www.sacredmysterytours.com/cathar-faith/
[520] http://www2.kenyon.edu/projects/margin/heresy.htm
[521] http://gnosis.org/library/Interrogatio_Johannis.html
[522] http://www.creme-de-languedoc.com/Languedoc/activities/sentier-cathar-trail.php

L'hérésie des bons homes [523]

Les hérésies, du XIIe au début du XIVe siècle [524]

Medieval Pure Ones [525]

Montségur and the Cathars [526]

Montségur: Identities of Cathars Executed on March 16, 1244 [527] [528]

Montségur: The Last Bastion of the Cathars [529]

---

[523] http://halshs.archives-ou-vertes.fr/docs/00/62/44/56/PDF/ThA_ry_L_hA_rA_sie_des_bons_hommes_Heresis_36-37_2002.pdf
[524] http://halshs.archives-ou-vertes.fr/docs/00/60/00/00/PDF/ThA_ry_HA_rA_sies_du_XIIe_au_dA_but_du_XIVe_s.pdf
[525] http://www.angelfire.com/ego/templar/page14.htm
[526] http://www.russianbooks.org/montsegur.htm
[527] http://www.russianbooks.org/montsegur/montsegur5.htm
[528] http://www.cathar.info/1211b_martyrdom.htm
[529] http://www.valeriebarrow.com/jehanne-darc/travels-to-sacred-places/montsegur-the-last-bastion-of-the-cathars.html

Raiders of the Lost Grail [530]

Secret Files of the Inquisition [531]

Secrets of the Cathars [532] [533] [534]

The 13 Things Dan Brown Didn't Tell You [535]

The Albigensian Crusade [536]

The Apareilementum [537]

530

http://www.forteantimes.com/features/articles/5407/raiders_
of_the_lost_grail.html
[531] http://www.pbs.org/inquisition/cathars.html
532

http://www.academia.edu/5187603/Secrets_of_the_Cathars
[533] http://wonderinspirit.wordpress.com/2012/02/19/secrets-
of-the-cathars/
534

http://www.bibliotecapleyades.net/esp_autor_whenry04.htm
[535] http://venturegalleries.com/blog/the-13-things-dan-
brown-didnt-tell-you/
[536] http://home.eckerd.edu/~oberhot/cathar.htm
[537] http://gnosis.org/library/appa.htm

Ad Infinitum: Unchanging and Forevermore

The Besieged and the Beautiful in Languedoc [538]

The Book of Two Principles [539]

The Cathar Prophecy of 1244 AD [540]

The Cathar Ritual (or Lyon Ritual) [541]

The Cathars [542] [543] [544] [545] [546] [547] [548] [549] [550]

---

[538]

http://www.nytimes.com/2010/05/09/travel/09Languedoc.html?_r=0

[539] http://gnosis.org/library/cathar-two-principles.htm

[540] http://wakinggiant.wordpress.com/2010/04/01/the-cathar-prophecy-of-1244-ad-the-fountain/

[541] http://gnosis.org/library/Cathar_Ritual-full_text.html

[542] http://www.forrester-roberts.co.uk/cathars.html

[543] http://www.bibliotecapleyades.net/esp_cataros.htm#menu

[544] http://raymondkhoury.com/the-last-templar/templars-cathars-and-the-jefferson-bible-behind-the-book/#sec7

[545] http://www.cathar.info/1209_inquisition.htm

[546] http://reluctant-messenger.com/cathars.htm

[547] http://www.ancientquest.com/embark/cathars.html

[548] http://www.mysticmissal.org/cathars.htm

[549] http://www.languedoc-france.info/articles/a_cathars.htm

[550] http://www.cathar.info/12011011_catharpater.htm

Ad Infinitum: Unchanging and Forevermore

The Cathars: The Struggle For and of A New Church [551]

The Consolamentum (Consolament) [552]

The Holy Land of Scotland [553]

The Inquisition Record of Jacques Fournier [554]

The Legacy of Liberation [555]

The Legend of the Cathars [556]

The Nazarene Way [557]

---

[551] http://www.philipcoppens.com/catharism.html
[552] http://gnosis.org/library/Consolamentum.html
[553] http://www.williamhenry.net/blog_scotland.html
[554]
http://www.sjsu.edu/people/nancy.stork/courses/c4/s1/jacqu
es_fournier
[555] http://gnosis.org/ecclesia/homily_Montsegur.htm
[556] http://www.wendag.com/forum/showthread.php/257-
The-Legend-of-the-Cathars
[557] http://www.thenazareneway.com/index.htm

The Other God [558]

The Trail of Gnosis (Judith Mann) [559]

The Voynich Manuscript and the Cathars of the Languedoc [560]

The War on the Cathars [561]

Traditio: Rite for the Transmission of the Prayer [562]

EDGAR CAYCE

Edgar Cayce's A.R.E. (Association for Research and Enlightenment) [563]

---

[558]

http://www.grahamhancock.com/forum/StoyanovYuri_Othe
rGod.php

[559] http://gnosistraditions.faithweb.com/tableofcontents.html

[560] http://www.languedocmysteries.info/voynich.htm

[561] https://www.newdawnmagazine.com/articles/the-war-on-
the-cathars

[562] http://gnosis.org/library/traditio.htm

[563] http://www.edgarcayce.org/

DAVID WILCOCK

Wilcock, David. *The Shift of the Ages: Convergence Volume One* (online book) [564]

Wilcock, David. *The Science of Oneness: Convergence Volume Two* (online book) [565]

Wilcock, David. *The Divine Cosmos: Convergence Volume Three* (online book) [566]

Wilcock, David. *Wanderer Awakening: The Life Story of David Wilcock* (online book) [567]

---

[564] http://divinecosmos.com/start-here/books-free-online/18-the-shift-of-the-ages
[565] http://divinecosmos.com/start-here/books-free-online/19-the-science-of-oneness
[566] http://divinecosmos.com/start-here/books-free-online/20-the-divine-cosmos
[567] http://divinecosmos.com/start-here/books-free-online/25-wander-awakening-the-life-story-of-david-wilcock

Wilcock, David. *The Reincarnation of Edgar Cayce* (online book) [568]

Wilcock, David. *The End of Our Century* (online book edited by David Wilcock) [569]

KING ARTHUR AND CAMELOT

A New Theory about King Arthur [570]

Arthurian Inscription [571]

Arthurian Resources and Studies [572]

Artúr mac Aedan of Dalriada [573]

---

[568] http://divinecosmos.com/start-here/books-free-online/22-the-reincarnation-of-edgar-cayce-draft-of-pt-1

[569] http://divinecosmos.com/start-here/books-free-online/26-the-end-of-our-century

[570] http://www.electricscotland.com/history/king_arthur.htm

[571] http://www.earlybritishkingdoms.com/articles/artstone.html

[572] http://www.arthuriana.co.uk/arthurian.htm

[573] http://www.heroicage.org/issues/1/haaad.htm

<u>Arturius: A Quest for Camelot</u>, [574] written by David F. Carroll, contains the irrefutable historical evidence of the existence of Arthur, who was none other than Arturius, son of Áedán mac Gabráin, King of the Dál Riata Scots (574 to 609 AD). [575] [576]

Britannia: Cadbury Castle – King Arthur's Camelot? [577]

Britannia: Early References to a Real Arthur [578]

Camelot [579]

Early Arthurian Tradition [580]

Evidence of the Existence of Arthur [581]

---

[574] http://kingarthurlegend.com/

[575] http://www.electricscotland.com/history/arturius.htm

[576] http://en.wikipedia.org/wiki/File:Dalriada.png

[577] http://www.britannia.com/history/arthur/cadcast.html

[578] http://www.britannia.com/history/arthur/karef.html

[579] http://www.grahamphillips.net/trail/3_camelot.htm

[580] http://www.mun.ca/mst/heroicage/issues/1/hatoc.htm

[581] http://www.kingarthurlegend.com/evidence-of-king-arthur.html

Faces of Arthur [582]

Historical Basis for King Arthur [583]

King Arthur in Early Welsh Literature [584]

King Arthur: The History, The Legend, The King [585]

The Iona Chronicle, the Descendants of Aedan mac Gabrain and the "Principal Kindreds of Dal Riata" [586]

The Kingdom of Manann [587]

---

[582] http://www.facesofarthur.org.uk/bibliograrth.htm
[583]
http://celtopedia.druidcircle.net/index.php?title=Historical_basis_for_King_Arthur
[584] http://www.britannia.com/history/docs/stanzas.html
[585] http://www.britannia.com/history/arthur/
[586] http://www.research.ed.ac.uk/portal/en/publications/the-iona-chronicle-the-descendants-of-aedan-mac-gabrain-and-the-principal-kindreds-of-dal-riata(8012da88-a45f-4783-bf31-a0b5fc60ae6f)/export.html
[587] http://www.kingarthurlegend.com/kingdom-of-manann.html

The Scottish Camelot [588]

Timeless Myths: Arthurian Legends [589]

KING HENRY IV OF FRANCE

French Wars of Religion [590]

Gabrielle D'Estrées [591] [592] [593]

Gabrielle D'Estrées, Marquise de Monceaux, Duchesse de Beaufort (1889) [594]

Henry IV [595] [596] [597] [598]

---

[588] http://www.britannia.com/history/arthur/camelon.html
[589] http://www.timelessmyths.com/arthurian/index.html
[590] http://en.wikipedia.org/wiki/French_Wars_of_Religion
[591]

http://gw.geneanet.org/genroy?lang=fr&p=gabrielle&n=d+e strees
[592] http://www.geneall.net/F/per_page.php?id=10543
[593]

http://gallica.bnf.fr/Search?ArianeWireIndex=index&p=1&l ang=FR&q=Gabrielle+d%27Estr%C3%A9es&x=14&y=9
[594] https://archive.org/details/gabrielledestr00descuoft
[595] http://www.henri-iv.com/index.htm

Henri IV – An Unfinished Reign [599]

Henry of Navarre (entire online movie 2010) [600]

Histoire d'amour de Gabrielle d'Estrées et de Henri IV [601]

Huguenots de France et d'ailleurs [602]

Le Roi Henri IV of France [603]

The Eclectic Magazine of Foreign Literature, Science and Art (1877) Volume 25 [604]

---

[596] http://www.biography.com/people/henry-iv-9335199#king-henry-iv&awesm=~oC259coUkW7eFC

[597] http://www.nndb.com/people/836/000093557/

[598] http://www.histoire-en-ligne.com/spip.php?article200

[599] http://www.henriiv.culture.fr/en/uc/00-Home#/en/uc/00

[600] https://www.youtube.com/watch?v=G_EqgerxUOw

[601] http://fra.1september.ru/view_article.php?ID=200900316

[602] http://huguenots-france.org/france.htm

[603] http://www.andreazuvich.com/history/le-roi-henri-iv-of-france/

[604] http://books.google.ca/books?id=JoTQAAAAMAAJ&pg=PA221&lpg=PA221&dq=chateau+de+coeuvres+%2B+Antoine+d%E2%80%99Estr%C3%A9es&source=bl&ots=RVzMaTxdm7&sig=pjibRlcDtayPl1oz4YmnxEPpQuQ&hl=en&sa

The Succession of Henri IV [605]

Wives and Mistresses of Henry IV [606]

LEMURIA (MU)

Admiral Byrd Diary [607] [608] [609]

A Short History of Lemuria [610]

Atlantis, Lemuria and Mu: Were They Real? [611]

=X&ei=juBLU7eWKsee2gXek4G4Dg&ved=0CEkQ6AEw
CQ#v=onepage&q=chateau%20de%20coeuvres%20%20%2
0Antoine%20d%E2%80%99Estr%C3%A9es&f=false
[605]

http://en.wikipedia.org/wiki/Henry_IV_of_France's_successi
on
[606]

http://en.wikipedia.org/wiki/Henry_IV_of_France's_wives_a
nd_mistresses
[607] http://www.admiralbyrddiary.com/
[608] http://www.phfawcettsweb.org/byrddiary.htm
[609] http://thehollowearthinsider.com/go-deeper/Site_-
_N_ew/Diary.html
[610] http://www.cybershaman.org/html/lemuria.html
[611] http://ancientaliensdebunked.com/atlantis-lemuria-and-
mu-were-they-real/

Different Theories About Lemuria [612]

Lemuria and Telos [613]

Lemuria: Fact or Fiction? [614]

Lemuria: The Continent of Mu [615]

Lemuria: The Hidden History of Mankind's Motherland (3 hour online video) [616]

Lemuria, the Land of Mu [617]

Mu (Lemuria) [618]

612

http://www.bibliotecapleyades.net/atlantida_mu/esp_lemuria _2.htm

613 http://www.lemurianconnection.com/category/about-lemuria-and-telos/

614 http://www.realhula.com/lemuria.html

615 http://www.bibliotecapleyades.net/esp_lemuria.htm

616 http://vimeo.com/4673696

617 http://www.burlingtonnews.net/leumurian1.html

618

http://www.edgarcayce.org/_AncientMysteriesTemp/mu.ht ml

The Inner Earth [619]

The Lost Lands of Mu and Lemuria [620]

The Law of One information base [621]

The Sacred Symbols of Mu [622]

The Search for the Lost Civilization of Mu Begins [623]

The Solar Brotherhood of the Seven Rays [624]

MEROVINGIAN KINGS

Burgundians in The Mist [625]

---

[619] http://www.thenewearth.org/InnerEarth.html
[620] http://www.redicecreations.com/article.php?id=1759
[621]

http://www.lawofone.info/results.php?q=+Lemuria+Mu&v=
r&sc=1
[622] http://sacred-texts.com/atl/ssm/index.htm
[623] http://www.barry.warmkessel.com/LEMURIA.html
[624] http://www.wolflodge.org/sananda/Brotherhood-
Rays.htm
[625] http://theburgundian.blogspot.ca/2010/03/marriage-of-
clovis-and-clotilda-story.html

Dark Ages and Merovingians [626]

Franks, Merovingian Kings [627]

List of Families Descending from the Merovingian and Carolingian Dynasties [628]

List of Frankish Kings [629]

Merovingian [630]

Merovingian Dynasty [631] [632]

---

[626] http://www.halexandria.org/dward216.htm

[627] http://fmg.ac/Projects/MedLands/MEROVINGIANS.htm

[628] http://www.eupedia.com/europe/families_descending_from_ charlemagne_clovis.shtml

[629] http://en.wikipedia.org/wiki/List_of_Frankish_kings

[630] http://www.princeton.edu/~achaney/tmve/wiki100k/docs/Me rovingian.html

[631] http://www.themolloys.net/molloy/france/merovingian%20d ynasty/merovingian%20dynasty.htm

[632] http://www.robertsewell.ca/merovingian.html

Merovingian Kings [633] [634] [635]

Sinclair DNA Maybe Not Merovingian DNA [636]

The Ancestors of Charlemagne: Addenda (1990) [637]

The DaVinci Code: Bloodlines [638]

The Frankish Empire [639]

The Kings and Queens of the Franks [640]

---

[633]
http://www.robertsewell.ca/pdf/030MerovingianKings.pdf
[634] http://www.lisashea.com/hobbies/art/merovingian.html
[635] http://mediaevalmusings.wordpress.com/2013/07/24/let-us-be-frank-the-merovingian-kings/
[636] http://www.stclairresearch.com/content/Sinclair-DNA-Merovingian.html
[637]
http://www.rootsweb.ancestry.com/~medieval/addcharlENG.pdf
[638] http://diggingforthetruth.net/season2episode10.html
[639] http://www.saylor.org/site/wp-content/uploads/2012/10/HIST201-1.1.1-FrankishEmpire-FINAL1.pdf
[640] http://www.ancient.eu.com/news/3574/

Ad Infinitum: Unchanging and Forevermore

The Merovingian Dynasty and the Grail Romances: A Medieval Mystery [641]

The Merovingian Long-Haired Kings [642]

The Merovingian Mythos [643]

The Merovingians [644] [645]

REINCARNATION

Can Science Uphold the Belief in Rebirth? [646]

[641] http://www.new-wisdom.org/cultural_history1/14-europe/1-merovingian.htm

[642] http://cynthiaripleymiller.wordpress.com/2013/07/27/france-the-merovingian-long-haired-kings/

[643] http://www.21stcenturyradio.com/merovingian-twyman.htm

[644] http://www.bibliotecapleyades.net/esp_merovingios.htm#menu

[645] http://www.rhedesium.com/the-merovingians-ndash-how-history-somehow-forgothellippart-one.html

[646] http://www.reversespins.com/singh.html

Children's Past Lives [647]

Could a Little Boy Be Proof of Reincarnation? [648]

Dr. Ian Stevenson: The Pioneer of Reincarnation Research [649]

Karma and Reincarnation [650]

Mellen-Thomas Benedict [651]

NDE: Arthur Yensen [652]

NDE: Dannion Brinkley [653]

---

[647] http://www.childpastlives.org/childrenspastlives.htm
[648] http://www.reversespins.com/proofofreincarnation.html
[649] http://www.near-death.com/experiences/reincarnation01.html
[650] http://www.himalayanacademy.com/resources/pamphlets/KarmaReincarnation.html
[651] http://www.mellen-thomas.com/
[652] http://www.near-death.com/experiences/reincarnation06.html
[653] http://www.near-death.com/experiences/evidence11.html

NDE: David Perry (1762) [654]

NDE: Jeanie Dicus [655]

NDE: Mellen-Thomas Benedict [656]

NDE: Thomas Sawyer [657]

Paul Gauguin and Peter Teekamp [658]

Reincarnation [659]

Reincarnation [660]

---

[654]

http://homepages.rootsweb.ancestry.com/~dagjones/docs/neardeath.html
[655] http://www.near-death.com/experiences/reincarnation05.html
[656] http://www.near-death.com/experiences/reincarnation04.html
[657] http://www.near-death.com/experiences/reincarnation03.html
[658] http://www.peterteekamp.com/summary.html
[659]

http://www.blavatsky.net/topics/reincarnation/reincarnation.htm
[660] http://www.reincarnation2002.com/

Reincarnation [661]

Reincarnation and the Early Christians [662]

Reincarnation and NDE Research [663]

Reincarnation Central [664]

Reincarnation in Christian History [665]

Reincarnation: Its Meaning and Consequences [666]

Return of the Revolutionaries: The Case for Reincarnation and Soul Groups Reunited [667]

Semkiw, Walter. (2011) *Born Again: Reincarnation Cases Involving Evidence of Past Lives with Xenoglossy Cases Researched by Ian Stevenson.*

---

[661] http://www.reincarnation.ws/
[662] http://www.near-death.com/experiences/origen06.html
[663] http://www.near-death.com/experiences/reincarnation02.html
[664] http://www.reincarnationcentral.com/sitemap.html
[665] http://www.near-death.com/experiences/origen08.html
[666] http://www.comparativereligion.com/reincarnation.html
[667] http://www.johnadams.net/

Scientific Proof of Reincarnation: Dr. Ian Stevenson's Life Work [668]

Shroder, Tom. (2001) *Old Souls: Compelling Evidence from Children Who Remember Past Lives.*

Statement of Reincarnation: Dalai Lama of Tibet [669]

Stevenson, Ian Dr. (1997) *Where Reincarnation and Biology Intersect.*

Stevenson, Ian Dr. (1997) *Reincarnation and Biology: A Contribution to the Etiology of Birthmarks and Birth Defects.*

Stevenson, Ian Dr. (1980) *Twenty Cases Suggestive of Reincarnation.*

Stevenson, Ian Dr. (2000) *Children Who Remember Previous Lives: A Question of Reincarnation.*

---

[668] http://reluctant-messenger.com/reincarnation-proof.htm
[669] http://dalailama.com/messages/tibet/reincarnation-statement

Someone Else's Yesterday [670]

The Boy Who Lived Before [671]

The Michael Newton Institute: For Life Between Lives Hypnotherapy [672]

The Question of Reincarnation, Part 1 [673]

The Question of Reincarnation, Part 2 [674]

The Question of Reincarnation, Part 3 [675]

The Reincarnation of Abraham Lincoln and John Fitzgerald Kennedy [676]

----

[670] http://www.confederateyankee.net/
[671]

http://www.reversespins.com/The_Boy_Who_Lived_Before
.html
[672] http://www.newtoninstitute.org/
[673] http://www.fst.org/reinc1.htm
[674] http://www.fst.org/reinc2.htm
[675] http://www.fst.org/reinc3.htm
[676] http://www.near-
death.com/experiences/reincarnation08.html

The Reincarnation Experiment: Paul Von Ward [677]

The Reincarnation of Jesus [678]

Tucker, Jim. (2008) *Life Before Life: Children's Memories of Previous Lives*.

Wynn Free Interview: The Reincarnation of Edgar Cayce [679]

WALES

Annals of Wales [680]

Historical King of the Britons [681]

Kings of Wales Family Trees [682]

---

[677] http://www.reincarnationexperiment.org/

[678] http://www.near-death.com/experiences/origen04.html

[679] http://www.peopleyoushouldmeet.com/index.php/wynn-free

[680] http://en.wikipedia.org/wiki/Annals_of_Wales

[681] http://en.wikipedia.org/wiki/King_of_the_Britons

[682]

http://en.wikipedia.org/wiki/Kings_of_Wales_family_trees

Legendary Kings of Britain [683]

Welsh Biography Online [684] [685]

683

http://en.wikipedia.org/wiki/List_of_legendary_kings_of_Br
itain
[684] http://www.culturenetcymru.com/en/?p=24
[685] http://wbo.llgc.org.uk/en/index.html

About the Author

Michele Doucette is webmistress of Portals of Spirit, a spirituality website whereby one will find links to categories of interest from Angels to Zen, books of spiritual resonance, videos and documentaries.

As a Level 2 Reiki Practitioner, she sends long distance Reiki to those who make the request, claiming only to be a facilitator of the Universal energy, meaning that it is up to the individual(s) in question to use these energies in order to heal themselves.

Having also acquired a Crystal Healing Practitioner diploma (Stonebridge College in the UK), she is guardian to many from the mineral kingdom.

She is the author of many spiritual (metaphysical) works; namely, [1] *The Ultimate Enlightenment For 2012: All We Need Is Ourselves*, a book that was nominated for the Allbooks Review Best Inspirational Book for 2011, [2] *Turn Off The TV: Turn On Your Mind*, [3] *Veracity At Its Best*,

[4] *The Collective: Essays on Reality* (a composition of essays in relation to the Matrix), [5] *Sleepers Awaken: The Time Is Now To Consciously Create Your Own Reality*, [6] *Healing the Planet and Ourselves: How To Raise Your Vibration*, [7] *You Are Everything: Everything Is You*, [8] *The Awakening of Humanity: A Foremost Necessity*, [9] *The Cosmos of the Soul: A Spiritual Biography*, [10] *Getting Out Of Our Own Way: Love Is The Only Answer*, [11] *Living The Jedi Way*, [12] *Vicarius Christi: The Vicar of Christ*, [13] *The Cosmos of the Soul II: Messages* and [14] *Living The ED Principles*, all of which have been published through St. Clair Publications. In addition, she has written a volume that deals with crystals, aptly entitled *The Wisdom of Crystals*.

She is also the author of *A Travel in Time to Grand Pré*, a visionary metaphysical novel that historically ties the descendants of Yeshua (Jesus) to modern day Nova Scotia. As shared by a reviewer, *Veracity At Its Best* "constructs the context for the spiritual message" imparted in *A Travel in Time to Grand Pré*.

Against the backdrop of 1754 Acadie, it was the blending of French Acadian history with current DNA testing that contributed to the weaving of this alchemical tale of time travel, romance and intrigue. From Henry I Sinclair to the Merovingians, from the Cathari treasure at Montségur to the Knights Templar, this novel, together with the words of Yeshua as spoken at the height of his ministry, has the potential to inspire others; for it is herein that we learn how individuals can find their way, their truth(s), in order to live their lives to the fullest.

Several years in the making, she was also driven to write *Back Home With Evangeline*, the sequel to *A Travel in Time to Grand Pré*.

It is here that Madeleine and Michel find themselves back in the twentieth century with a message that must be shared with the world. So, too, and even more importantly, must the message be lived, and experienced, by one and all.

So, too, is she the author of *Time Will Tell*, a uniquely moving tale that begins in the present day before weaving its way backward through time to connect a glowing thread of historic discoveries. Courtesy of past-life regression, Michaela (Dr. Mike) Callaghan, a brilliant metaphysical scientist, in the twenty-first century, discovers that she lived as a young, noble, Cathari herbalist healer, in the Languedoc area of France, during a time when political change was in the air.

When not working as a Special Education teacher, she continues to read, research and write, exploring her personal genealogies, all of which constitute her passion.

In the words of the Dalai Lama ... *In order to be happy, one must first possess inner contentment; and inner contentment cannot come from having all we want; rather it comes from having and appreciating all we have.*

www.ingramcontent.com/pod-product-compliance
Lightning Source LLC
Chambersburg PA
CBHW060548260626
47161CB00003B/1098